AN ISLAND FOR TWO

Also by Ludek Pesek
THE EARTH IS NEAR

AN ISLAND FOR TWO
By Ludek Pesek

Translated from the German by Anthea Bell

BRADBURY PRESS   SCARSDALE, NEW YORK

Set me as a seal upon thine heart . . .

THE SONG OF SOLOMON 8:6

It began just before eight on the evening of Saturday 24 June, 1972, the last day of the sale at Mooser's department store in the Bahnhofstrasse in Zürich. A young man, accompanied by a girl, came out of the old, four-storeyed building by the back way. The man's thick beard looked scuffy; so did his tangled, greasy, shoulder-length dark hair. He was wearing faded blue jeans, which fitted tightly around his thin hips, a red and gray check shirt, and worn-out sandals. A canvas bag on a short strap dangled from his left shoulder. His shabby imitation-leather jacket was slung over his right hand, which held his companion's elbow close to his own body.

The girl's hair was long as well, but hers was fair, well brushed and shining. Her short black skirt was immaculate. Her gleaming shiny-look shoes were spotless too, and her white blouse stood out in the evening twilight. None of this was an unusual sight in the streets of Zürich. The only unusual thing was the expression in the girl's eyes, a mixture of fear and something indefinable. She was a head shorter than the man, and could hardly keep up as he strode along. She was

I

not going with him voluntarily. There was a pistol pressing into her left ribs; the young man was holding it in his right hand beneath the leather jacket.

At this time of day, the city streets were full of indifferent passers-by, all going somewhere in a hurry.

Four hours later, at about midnight, mid-European time, a nuclear warhead was exploded on an island in the Pacific Ocean. It was a routine nuclear test, conducted well away from any inhabited area.

Part One

I

He kept her elbow pressed hard against his hip, afraid
she might tear herself free and run away. Fear and
nervousness constricted his chest, and his breath came
fast and shallow. He felt as though this was all just a
dream, but he could feel the metal of the pistol in his
hand, wet with sweat beneath the jacket, and he pulled
the girl's soft arm close against his thin ribs. He was
in a hurry to reach the old Volkswagen he had parked
near the Münsterbrücke three hours before. He had it
all worked out in advance; the walk took just four
minutes, but now the short distance seemed intermi-
nable. Scenes flashed through his mind like random clips
from a film. Nothing consecutive; he was too agitated.
However, it had been worse a fortnight ago.

A fortnight ago, he had been sitting on the ground
behind some packing cases holding refrigerators on the
fourth floor of Mooser's, in the corridor leading to
Accounts, feeling so nervous that he was breathless
even though he was sitting quite still. Mentally, he kept
rehearsing the words he was going to say when he
walked into the Accounts office, pistol in hand, the
stocking mask over his head. The safe was in there. He

had prepared a brief sentence to be spoken in German with an English accent. He intended to speak bad German on purpose to mislead the cops. He was proud of this idea. It was a very short sentence, yet suddenly he could not remember the exact words. He, imagined himself standing there masked, pistol in hand, stammering something unintelligible. It was quiet behind the packing cases, but there was a loud rumbling in his guts. Sweat dripped from his face, and the pistol in his hand felt wet. Soon the spasms in his guts became so acute that he had to leave his hiding place and slip away. He had diarrhoea. The hold-up was postponed for a week.

All this was flashing through his mind in disjointed fragments, mixed up with a mental picture of the book-keeper's horrified face, of the bundles of banknotes rustling as they fell into the canvas bag. Then there were other fragments: the face of an elderly woman clerk, distorted by fear, and then a young face framed in golden hair. Out of the corner of his eye, he could see that hair beside him now.

A week ago, there had been no tall packing cases in the corridor at all. A week ago, he had been badly disappointed. He wanted to get it over and done with. He had never read a magazine story where a gangster had to postpone a hold-up because he had diarrhoea, or the crates he was going to use as cover had been taken away the day before. Come to that, he had never read a story about a gangster who stammered during a hold-up. He was furious: furious with the fools who make up the gangster stories, furious with the whole world, because he was not sleeping well these days, and now he could expect bad nights for another whole week.

But today it had worked. Everything had gone according to plan. Or had it? He had a vague presentiment that his real troubles were only just beginning. He was going to need quite as much luck as he'd had so far. He wiped his left shirt sleeve over his sweaty face; he was still sweating profusely. No, of course it had not gone according to plan . . . crouching behind those packing cases half an hour ago, he had felt the sweat flowing from his armpits, trickling down his ribs under his shirt, all the way down to his belt, while he heard his innards rumbling. Suddenly, half an hour ago, he'd wanted to drop the whole thing. But he hated to give up. The Home had trained him well in that, if nothing else; experience had taught him that he never regretted the things he had actually done, only those he had failed to do. Time passed desperately slowly. The wood of the packing cases had a funny smell, a smell that reminded him of something. It was a memory he was always trying to thrust to the back of his mind, but now and then it would creep inexorably up on him. He had been hiding behind packing cases then too, and he had been bathed in sweat. Fat Minna! Maybe she wasn't quite all there, but she was bright enough at some things. The smell of the wooden packing cases brought back a picture of her fat, naked thighs, and the sparse hair below her plump white stomach. Why did he have to go and remember that just now? Mentally, he rehearsed his words. "This is a hold-up. Hands up! Don't move, or I shoot!" He was afraid his hand might tremble. But after a while, when the sweat had cooled and evaporated, another person seemed to take possession of his shivering, tense body. He observed this change in surprise. He watched himself calmly pull the stocking mask over his head and face, pick up the pistol, cover his hand with his jacket, and step firmly out of his hiding place.

Then everything unreeled like a speeded-up film. It went so fast that only an abbreviated, indistinct sketch of it remained. He had, in fact, made rather a hash of his carefully rehearsed speech. He spoke in a nasal tone, because the stocking over his face got in the way of his lips. But the pistol was effective enough. It made them terrified and submissive. Office hours were over long ago, and there were only four people there in Accounts: the short-sighted, bald bookkeeper, two elderly women clerks, and a trainee helping with the pay packets. Mooser's was a solid, old-fashioned firm, and old-fashioned trust was the order of the day for its employees. He was quite surprised to find how smoothly it all went. He had probably managed to get right down from the fourth floor with his hostage before anyone in the office plucked up courage to move. He was in such a state of excitement that he nearly ran out into the street with the stocking still over his head, but he tore it off at the last moment, just before they reached the doorway.

Now, hurrying toward the car with his hostage, he was calming down. He thought the girl seemed calmer too; he no longer feared she might break into hysterical screams.

At the end of the block, not fifty meters from his Volkswagen, he stopped short, his heart in his mouth. For a few moments he stood there, irresolute. Sweat broke out on his forehead.

"Bloody hell," he said softly, clamping his prisoner's elbow tightly against his hip.

They stood side by side in silence, breathing hard; they did not look at each other. She was staring at the ground. He put the canvas bag of money down on the pavement, propping it against his leg, and wiped his sweaty face with the back of his left hand. Then, picking up the bag, he pushed the pistol harder into the girl's ribs and said, "Just keep your mouth shut." They were the first words he had spoken to her. He led her toward an old Volkswagen with rusty bumpers and a number plate stolen in München.

There was a policeman standing on the pavement beside the car.

2

"This your car?" asked the policeman brusquely, as the man and girl stopped beside the shabby car.

"That's right," the young man croaked. His voice would not obey him.

"I suppose you know your back tires are almost bald?"

"I was just going to get some new ones . . ."

"I can't let you go on with these, see? Interests of public safety. Your own safety too," said the policeman, speaking with all the superiority of an official who knows he has the law on his side.

"But . . . but that's a disaster!" said the young man, in tones of genuine despair.

The policeman's eyes wandered over the battered car, and then over the youth's faded jeans. He went on, in a slightly different voice, "That's a Münich number plate. You from Münich?"

" 'Sright," said the young man despondently.

"Where are you going, then?"

"Home. First thing tomorrow," he said, a little more brightly.

"Hm. I shouldn't really . . ." The policeman hesitated. "Still—look, you get out of here, quick as you can. And go and buy those tires, right? In your own interests."

Wiping the sweat from his forehead with the back of his left hand, the young man tried to smile. The policeman, thinking the long-haired youth's voice and expression denoted respect and confusion, began to feel benevolent. He might feel called upon to act suitably as the official representative of law and order, but plainly he had no personal objection to long hair or girls in tight skirts . . . the way he tried, and failed, to keep his eyes from wandering over the girl's long, slim legs was obvious.

"Sure!" said the young man fervently. "I'll get the tires changed tomorrow." He opened the car door for the girl, and slammed it shut the moment she sat down. Then he wrenched open the door on the other side, slung the canvas bag on the back seat, and got behind the wheel. The pistol was still in his right hand, hidden by the leather jacket.

The policeman stood on the pavement, watching the young man's haste to move off with approval.

"Thanks, sir! Thanks a lot!" The young man forced a smile. He did not know what to do about the pistol.

The policeman seemed to have no immediate intention of turning away. Instead, he approached the window, which was wound half-way down, with a friendly smile.

Putting the pistol and his jacket down in the space between the two front seats, the young man started the car. Still smiling, the policeman held up the traffic to allow the Volkswagen to get out of the parking place. As they drove past him, the youth waved. The girl was looking straight ahead, her eyes expressionless.

The Volkswagen's engine stalled several times. The young man drove on to the bridge, and then turned right along the quay. The Saturday evening traffic was heavy, and he wasted no time in talking. Now and then he wiped his sweaty face with a dirty handkerchief. The idea of being involved in some accident gave him the jitters.

"Where are you taking me?" the girl asked quietly, as they stopped for the red lights at the Bellevue crossing.

He did not reply, but drummed nervously on the wheel with his fingers. When the lights changed to green he drove on, getting into the lane for Rapperswil. The noisy old Volkswagen began to go better along the Seestrasse, when they were past the last traffic lights and out into the suburbs. Its engine was clattering like a threshing machine. The noise reassured the young man; his tense face relaxed.

"Should've knocked him off. The shit!" he said. He felt an urge to swear. "Swiss bastard—I bet he took my number."

The sky was clouded over, and in the dim evening light people were beginning to switch on their car lights. Other lights were coming on in the windows of villas and houses on the slopes along the road which runs along the side of the Lake of Zürich. The sight of all those quiet, happy homes seemed to depress the girl; she looked miserable sitting there, moving only to tug her short skirt down toward her knees now and then, with an automatic gesture. Apparently she didn't dare repeat her question to her kidnapper.

He was silent too. As the engine rattled and clattered, he was wondering how he could get rid of his hostage as soon as possible—though that would muck up his original plan. He realized he was beginning to feel sorry for the girl. He stole a glance at her profile from time to time. Yes, he was beginning to get much too interested in her, and that was no part of his plan; it just made things complicated. If only he'd taken the old biddy along . . . the situation would have been much simpler! Well, yes, but for Christ's sake, would he have been able to take the old girl's arm and stroll down a crowded pavement with her? She'd have gone into hysterics on the spot!

He thought about the money in the bag. How much was it really? He tried to estimate the amount, but found he couldn't concentrate. He could not resist the temptation to cast an occasional glance at his companion. As they approached Rapperswil, he said, "Don't worry. Nothing's going to happen to you."

He tried to make his voice as reassuring as possible, though he had to shout above the noise of the laboring engine. The girl turned her face toward him in surprise, and smiled very slightly. He looked briefly into her eyes for the first time. At the identical moment, he remembered the money, and turned cold. This girl, in actual fact, was his worst enemy. The moment she was out of the car she'd run for the nearest telephone and spill it all to the cops . . . the bastards. Everything she knew. No weakening, he told himself. No feeling sorry for anyone. Did anyone ever feel sorry for me?

Soon after they were through Rapperswil, the girl suddenly said, "Would you stop somewhere, please?"

"You don't get away that easily!" he said roughly.

Beyond the Rapperswil embankment he turned off

13

toward Einsiedeln. Soon they had left the houses behind. The surrounding landscape was fading into the
twilight; there were grassy slopes, surmounted by
woods, on both sides of the road now. The old car was
having difficulty getting up the long slope.

When they were on a flat stretch of road again, and
the engine was quieter, the girl repeated her request.
"Please, would you stop somewhere for a moment?" She
looked as if she were going to cry. She turned her face
away from the driver and stared out of the car window
at the countryside, hazy in the evening light.

The lights of the few scattered houses looked peaceful. He raised his foot off the accelerator slightly, and
the engine noise eased up.

"Want to have a pee?" His voice was cold and im-
personal.

"Yes." Hers was equally cold.

He said no more, but drove on for a while, and then
stopped near a thicket between two fields.

"No tricks, mind. Don't go trying anything!" He
spoke harshly.

They both got out, and he followed her, pistol in
hand, feeling a bit embarrassed. He didn't know just
how to deal with this situation. It was not the kind of
thing he'd allowed for when he made his plan. She
heard him following her, and stopped.

"But you . . . you can't . . ." she began, in tones
of mingled embarrassment and desperation. It sounded
as if she were on the brink of tears again.

He hesitated.

"I'll give you my word of honor," she said.

"What d'you mean?" he asked, not understanding
her.

"My word of honor not to run away."

He stood there for a moment, then turned, went back to the car, got in and put the pistol down on the floor. He rested his hands on the steering wheel and stared at the bright streaks of sky, gleaming like mother-of-pearl among the dark rainclouds in the west.

"You damn fool!" he told himself under his breath. "Letting that little bitch trick you so easily." He wondered how much longer he dared go on driving. Half an hour, at the outside. It would take that damn blonde half an hour to reach a telephone somewhere, and he must get off the road before then.

He switched the engine on and looked at his wristwatch. Just as he put his foot down on the clutch and was reaching for the gear lever, he saw the girl coming back through the gathering dusk.

She opened the car door, wriggled into the seat, smoothed her skirt down, and closed the door again. He did not know what to say. He did not know whether to say anything at all. He felt enormous relief. Looking at her face, in the rosy glow of the headlamps reflected from the road, he broke into loud and boyish laughter.

3

After this they both talked more. She asked what he would have done if he had seen her running off over the fields.

"I wouldn't have been able to shoot you," he said, honestly, and corrected himself hastily. "Though of course I would, in certain circumstances."

She asked, "What circumstances?"

"Never mind," he said. "Don't be so serious. I'd rather see you laugh!"

"I've got nothing to laugh about."

"I've already told you, nothing's going to happen to you. Look, I just want to get as far as I can. This is my own affair. I'm sorry you had to be dragged into it." After a brief pause he added, "Not married, are you?"

"No," she said.

"I suppose your parents will be worried?"

"Could be. I've really no idea." Her voice was cool.

Rather surprised, he turned his head, trying to make out the expression on her face in the dim light. "Why? Something the matter with your parents?"

She did not reply, and he tried to probe further. "Separated, I bet. Right?"

Still she said nothing; she was not inclined to be communicative on the subject. He tried another tack.

"Do you have a lot of . . ." He had been going to say "boy friends," but even before the word was out he realized it was a stupid question. Anyway, what the hell did it have to do with him? I'll be putting you out in the forest in an hour's time, he thought, and two hours later I'll have forgotten all about you. What do I care for you? Maybe you've got a bald old sugar daddy somewhere. The world's full of shit; money and sex, everything hinges on money and sex. It stinks. He felt emptiness and disappointment welling up inside him. He knew that feeling; it started up whenever he thought about Käthe. Käthe was blonde, like this girl. Another blonde! When he thought of Käthe, other experiences came back to him as well, things he didn't like to remember. There was the time long ago, when he was eleven or twelve, and Siggi had brought a little book to school. Siggi Hoffmann, with the sticking-out ears. Siggi read out whole passages from this book in the toilets during break. It was about some couple making love, and full of exciting words and ideas. Siggi's big ears went scarlet as he read, and the stink of the school toilets was superimposed on the descriptions of love-making.

Afterwards, he had never been able to keep the ideas of love-making and filth apart. Once, at night, a noise of some kind had waked him. He got off the old sofa in the kitchen, where he slept, and crawled quietly over to the door in the dark. He wanted to hear what Uncle Paul was saying about the Home. He had heard Uncle Paul mention this Home before, and his aunt had cried, and said she could never do such a thing, and her sister would turn in her grave. Then Uncle Paul got angry. "And why the hell should *I* take in her bastard?" He was drunk, the same as every Saturday, and though he was trying to keep his voice down it boomed as if it came from inside a beer barrel. "He's no kin of mine. I'm not having him here, and that's that!" It was easy to hear every word, even when the door was closed . . . but tonight the door was not quite closed, and Uncle Paul was not saying things in his hoarse, beery voice either. He was groaning instead, and the bedstead was creaking. Aunt Liese was moaning too, and whispering, "Pupi, oh Pupi, Pupi . . ." He had never heard her call Uncle Paul "Pupi" before. He'd never heard her moan like that before. "Oh, Pupi, oh, oh . . ." The room was full of a mysterious, hoarse darkness, and he knelt on the floor by the door, trembling with a strange kind of excitement. Then he heard his uncle's rough, hoarse voice: "Blasted beer . . . hold on a minute . . . got to have a pee . . ."

"What's the matter with you?" the girl asked.

With difficulty, he brought himself back to the present. "What do you mean?"

"Aren't you feeling well?"

"Why wouldn't I be?"

"You're breathing like . . . like . . ." She didn't know like what.

Recovering himself, he began to laugh—the clear, boyish laugh again. "Breathing like what?" he asked. "Like an animal or something?"

They both laughed. "How many times have you held people up before?" she asked.

"This is the fifth time," he said. "No, wait a moment, the sixth! I forgot that traffic warden I stabbed. Only got a hundred-franc note out of that one."

"This is the first time," she said, with certainty. "And the last."

"Jesus Christ!" he sighed in mock horror. "Brought your crystal ball along, have you?"

However, she did not laugh. It was as if she were trying to convince herself of something that she really wanted to believe. "No, honestly, real bandits look quite different."

"How *do* they look, then?"

"Brutal. Well, I don't mean like a gorilla or anything. But you can tell from their eyes."

"And what can you tell from mine?"

"Not much," she said truthfully. "Except that they're gray. I was glad when you took that mask off. You looked horrible before. But when I saw what you really looked like, I told myself criminals don't look like that."

"Christ! You from the Salvation Army? You'll be the death of me!" he said with forced amusement. He felt his position was being subtly threatened, and it was not pleasant to feel himself going on the defensive. He wasn't going to stand for being preached at by a . . . a . . . well, a girl who'd tumble into bed with some randy old man. Pretty girls are all tarts . . . and blondes are the worst of the lot. He tried to keep his mind on the money in the canvas bag, but he was feeling too restless. If those were all hundred-franc notes, it would be a lot. But that old fool had begun by putting twenties and fifties into the bag. Still, it must come to around twenty thousand, at least. Maybe a hundred thousand? Christ, he didn't need that much! Suddenly he took fright—surely this was all a nightmare? He put his left hand into his pocket for his crumpled, damp handkerchief, and wiped his face. No, it wasn't a dream this time. This was real. Which made it much simpler than any dream. He was amazed to find how simple reality was. But then he recognized the emotion which was making him shake all over from time to time. It was fear. He saw the smiling face of the Swiss policeman in the parking place. How does a policeman's face look when he's arresting you? "The son of a bitch," he muttered, wrenching the wheel violently to the right. The tires squealed on the asphalt, the car swerved and all but went into the ditch on the left of the highway. The girl, thrown against the side of the car by the centrifugal force, made a grab for the door handle, missed it, and fell against the driver.

"Sorry," he said coolly.

She sat up, tried to pull her skirt further down, and tossed her long hair back over her shoulder with a practiced movement. He was silent, thinking what luck it had been that there was nothing coming in the opposite direction. He realized how much a moment's carelessness could cost him. He felt furious with the smiling policeman who had threatened to wreck his whole beautiful plan. He'd have to step on it now.

"That Swiss bastard," he said, his voice audible above the groaning, screeching and laboring of the run-down old engine.

"You don't like the Swiss, do you." said the girl, after a moment. It was a statement rather than a question.

"The Swiss are all morons," he said. "They're all rich, and all rich people are morons. It's a law of nature. Degeneration of the species."

"I'm Swiss, but I'm not rich. So does that make me a moron?"

He gave an edgy laugh. "You can't put it that crudely."

"*You* put it that crudely."

"Christ, what a problem!" he said. "Look, you've got no idea what I mean. You don't understand the first thing about it."

"You've got nothing against Swiss francs, though, have you?"

He laughed again; it was not the boyish laugh this time. After a while he asked, "Ever thought much about Tahiti?"

The sudden change of subject bewildered her.

"Why Tahiti? What's Tahiti got to do with anything?"

"Well, it doesn't necessarily have to be Tahiti. Any island. Nothing but sand and palm trees, and the sea and the clouds and so on."

"I've been to Mallorca. And the Canary Islands, on a Kuoni tour. But there are crowds of people there, and not many palm trees."

"That's why I asked if you'd ever thought about Tahiti."

"Oh, I see what you mean. The romantic solitude bit. Only I bet there are even more people in Honolulu than Teneriffe."

"For God's sake, Honolulu isn't on Tahiti!" he said impatiently. "It's on Hawaii. And full of rich morons too. But have you ever thought about the kind of island I mean?"

"Not in my line!" she said dryly. "I'm not romantic. No, I never *have* thought about an island like that. Not even when I was only just getting to be a big girl!"

His face darkened; he felt he had been maneuvered

on to the defensive again. She's getting above herself, he thought. Rich Mummy and Daddy's little pet, obviously. Mallorca—the Canaries! A Swiss girl, and poor! Daddy will be getting her a job in a bank one of these fine days, nice and close to all that lovely money. That's the Swiss for you. Daddy's little girl will hang about, getting bored, till she marries some rich old goat. Blonde by nature, that's her. "It's no good talking to you about that sort of thing," he said bitterly. "You're blonde by nature, you are."

"What's that supposed to mean?" she asked, a trace of bitterness in her own voice. "Feeble, or something?"

He did not reply.

Obviously, his remark had hurt her. She was trying to justify herself somehow. Or was it that she'd only just discovered what she was really like?

Deep in thought, she said, "I suppose I *am* romantic, though. If I weren't I'd have run away from you, a quarter of an hour ago."

Once past Biberbruck, the road began to climb toward Sattel. The western horizon, above the wooded heights, was a cold, pale green. The road was deserted. Then two tiny lights appeared in the driving mirror. They unnerved the young man; he found he was wiping his wet palms on his trousers every now and then. As the lights grew larger in the mirror, he contemplated stopping, grabbing the bag of money and running for the dark wood which loomed up beyond the meadow at the roadside. The engine was laboring as the car climbed, and he had to shift down. The old Volkswagen dragged itself wearily on. The young man was breathing as if he himself were making a physical effort, or as if he could make the car go faster by sheer will-power.

He spotted a path across the fields to the right of the road, and turned into it without stopping to think. Though they had been going slowly, the girl lost her balance again and fell against the driver, but this time he did not apologize. He drove a short way and then stopped. Feverishly, he groped for the pistol, which was somewhere on the floor. When he found it, he thrust it into his trouser pocket and flung the car door open.

"What's happening?" asked the girl, her voice choked with fright.

He leaned over the back seat and reached for the bag, which had slipped to the floor as they drove. Just as he was hauling the bag out of the car, the headlamps of a large vehicle lit up the road with white light. It was a fast, powerful American car; it had come up faster than the young man expected. However, it swept past them and zoomed on into the darkness. The big red rear lights began to get smaller. Judging by the shape of them, it was a Cougar.

"Moron!" he said hoarsely. "Goddam plutocratic moron!"

He got back into the car and closed the door. Then he backed on to the empty road. The old Volkswagen moved off, its worn valves clattering like an old sewing-machine.

"When are you going to drop me off?" asked the girl. "It'll soon be night."

"All in good time," he said coldly. "When I feel like it."

4

He tried to think about the money again, and again he failed. The thing that prevented him was sitting on the seat beside him. Only it was not a thing, but a girl. In his plan—the plan he had considered so well thought out—it had been just a thing, a hostage. A kind of safety device. But now it was different. What was more, the hostage didn't look the way he had imagined the hostage in his plan. He was annoyed that she had turned out to be a pretty young girl. He supposed he ought to have been pleased, but he was not. In particular, because he couldn't manage to be as ruthless as he wanted, which in itself endangered the success of the whole affair. After it had begun so well! You fool, he told himself, she'll set the very first cop she meets on to you, and here you sit bothering about her feelings!

"Can I ask you a favor?" she said, so quietly that she was barely audible above the noise of the engine.

He did not reply. He could have wished she had been shrill and hostile; then it would have been easier not to bother about her feelings.

"I left my cigarettes in the office, in my handbag. I need a cigarette badly," she said softly.

24

"No luck. I don't smoke," he said brusquely. "No booze, no pot, no sleeping around; I just hold people up, that's all."

She did not reply, and her silence exasperated him. "I'm not a hippie, see?" he said with unnecessary force. "I don't need any filthy drugs to get me out of this stinking hole and transport me to Paradise, and all that. I can do just fine without Jesus Christ too. Hell, why go turning the other cheek? I used to get clouted on both cheeks when I was no more than that high. All *I* need is the cash, see?"

She was taken aback by his sudden bitterness, and waited for some time before asking, "Do you really want to go to Tahiti?"

He did not reply. He was busy observing his own lapse into communicativeness with horror and dismay. What the hell was the matter with him? What were his nerves doing, playing him up like this? Jesus, what *else* am I going to find myself telling this little tart . . . ? It'll be just like that other time . . . For the journey to some distant and dimly perceived Paradise had begun long ago. Twelve years ago. In the Home near Düsseldorf where Uncle Paul had put him. It was warm in the Home, and there was enough to eat, and he didn't have to sleep on a worn-out sofa with its springs digging into his back, but he did not like it there. He longed for his corner in the kitchen like a cat longing for its old home. He'd happily have put up with the drunken row Uncle Paul made every Saturday night, when he came home enveloped in a thick cloud of beer fumes. But he was afraid of Uncle Paul's anger, and his heavy hand, and he knew there was no appealing against his decision. Uncle Paul.

Paul-Pupi. He was afraid of the Head of the Home too; the Head's stern and military bearing terrified the boy. He decided to run away. Exactly where he was going he didn't know, but he knew it would be somewhere very far away. That was his secret, and he carried it around with him night and day, until he found the burden so appallingly heavy that he had to tell someone, anyone.

"I'm getting out of here," he told Ossi. He had picked Oswald Horowitz as his confidant because Ossi was small and weak, and would, he knew, have liked to run away too.

"Where are you going?" asked Ossi, an expression of mingled alarm and admiration on his thin face, with its slightly protuberant eyes. Ossi always looked rather poorly, and there was always something the matter with his throat.

"That's a secret. It's a very long way off, and anyone who tried to come after me would die a horrible death."

"Take me with you!" Ossi begged.

"No." It was a very definite refusal. He was not fond of small, weak creatures. He wanted to grow big and strong himself, and then he need not be afraid of Uncle Paul. He enjoyed seeing the bitter disappointment in Oswald Horowitz's eyes. Indeed, that was why he had picked Ossi; he wanted to torment him. He told Ossi an imaginary story about a rich uncle, who owned a white steamship and an island in the sea, with pineapples growing all over it. He had invented all sorts of details, and he wished, fiercely, that they were true. The longer he talked about them, the more he felt that they *were* true. He was sure such an island did exist.

"And if you tell, *you'll* die a horrible death," he threatened.

He basked in the visible terror and disappointment on Ossi's face. Oswald Horowitz was even smaller and more wretched than he was himself.

Ossi asked him once or twice more after that to take him along to the island where pineapples grew, and each time he refused. Well, he had to refuse; he didn't want Ossi discovering how very, very far away the island really was.

Then, one evening, he was summoned to the Head's room. The Head got down to business at once.

"So you're getting out of here, eh?" And he preached a long sermon, all about discipline. The world was a barracks. He did not listen to what the Head was saying. He was longing to be somewhere very far away. So Oswald Horowitz had told tales! The little bastard! And he'd been going to let him come too!

He ran away next day, first thing in the morning. He reached Düsseldorf on foot. By afternoon, he was so hungry that he stole a piece of sausage from a supermarket. He managed to slip out into the street and lose himself in the crowd. He ate the sausage in a dark corner of the empty waiting-room at the station; he could not help feeling that a stolen sausage must look different from a bought one, and he was glad when he had disposed of it.

The police got him just as he was scrambling into a delivery truck, and a policeman took him back to the Home. When the policeman had gone, the Head clipped him over the ear, saying that was just a little sample of what he could expect if he tried anything like that again.

However, he did run away again, three times. Once he even managed to steal a ride on the train to Hamburg. But hunger was his undoing; it was when he tried to satisfy his hunger by pilfering from supermarkets that things went wrong, every time. He went on from the Home to an approved school, where the discipline was stricter. The idea was that community life of this sort would be good for his character. However, he was already a confirmed individualist by now, and all the approved school did for him was teach him that you must be powerful to break out of a cage. And the older he grew, the more convinced he became of the power of money. If you had money, you could do anything you wanted. You needed money to get to somewhere very far away. Yes, he'd learned a lot. When he was fourteen he started work as an apprentice motor mechanic. He knew that motor mechanics earned a lot of money, and as yet he had no idea just how much money you really need in order to be powerful.

The headlamps of the car lit up the tree-trunks on both sides of the road through the wood. To the left, there were piles of timber, carefully stacked in the tidy Swiss fashion. The stacks of wood told him he was approaching the fork in the road that he had found over a fortnight ago. He had driven over the route once at night, too, so as to be absolutely sure of finding it again. Yet now, the closer he came to the place, the less able he felt to carry out his plan. About a hundred meters further on, he turned off the road and on to a rough path, deeply rutted by the tires of a tractor and trailer. The tree-trunks reflected the light of the headlamps back into the car, and in that light he saw the girl reach for the door handle.

"Stop fooling about!" he said angrily. "Want to cripple yourself for life? I told you, nothing's going to happen to you."

He drove on, slowly and carefully; the going was rough. The car jolted and squeaked. In the silence of the wood, the roaring of the engine seemed indecently loud, but in spite of that he could hear that the girl was crying. Not loud, healing, liberating tears; her weeping was quiet and convulsive, the tears were choking her. Everything they should be washing away was still there inside her.

"God!" he said bitterly. "Can't you trust me, just for a little? I trusted you back there!"

The only answer was more convulsive sobbing. That was about all he'd needed! Hysteria! The hell with pity. Or was it sympathy he felt?

He drove on, more and more slowly, until finally he stopped altogether, switched off the engine and stared irresolutely into the beams of the headlamps. Some moths were fluttering about in them. Then he switched off the lights and spoke into the darkness.

"I was going to get rid of you here," he said. There was suppressed anger in his voice, and an odd kind of disappointment. "I wasn't going to leave you free to run off, of course. I need time. I was going to tie my hostage to a tree, so I could be sure I'd be safe till morning. But I can't. Bloody hell, I can't do that to you. What a fool I am!" he added bitterly.

She was crying noisily now; nervous tension had broken through her self-control. He went on, as if he were thinking out loud: "So suppose I let you go. Here, or a little further on. What do you do then? No, I can tell you what. You run straight to the nearest light and the nearest telephone you can find. Then you describe the bandit to the police, so the bastards can get after him. As good as a photograph, it'll be."

The sky was clouded over; there was velvety black darkness in the wood. The girl tried to say something, but her nose was stuffed up with her tears, and she was sobbing too hard to draw breath. He wanted to speak roughly, but instead he found himself saying, in subdued tones, "Hell, don't cry. I'm a goddam fool, but I tell you what I'll do. I'll drive you to Brunnen, to the station, and you can catch the night train back to Zürich. But you don't go to the police till morning, okay? Promise? Give me your word of honor?"

After several attempts, she managed to utter, between her sobs, "I promise!"

He put his hand into his pocket for his handkerchief, the one he had used to wipe the sweat from his face as he drove, and pushed it into her hand in the dark. "Here, blow your nose! I can't make you out at all."

She obediently took the handkerchief, and blew her nose violently. He sighed, then switched on the engine and the lights.

"We can't turn here. But there's a wooden bridge a little further on, and a place the other side where the path forks—I'll turn there. Promise!"

He drove slowly on. The girl blew her nose a couple more times, but it was quite a gentle sound against the noise of the engine.

The little bridge appeared in the light of the headlamps. It crossed a ravine, with water gleaming on the rocks below. On the other side of the bridge, the path forked. The young man stopped here, leaving the lights on, and got out of the car. He examined the muddy ground carefully; the ruts were deep, and he did not want to get stuck as he turned. He walked twice across the spot where the path forked, testing the ground with his foot to see just how soft it was. In the glare of the headlamps he looked like the villain in some amateur theatrical production, with his tangled long hair and bushy beard. But the girl sitting in the car knew that this was not a play. She could see the shape of the pistol on his right thigh, where the pocket of his tight jeans would be.

He got back into the car. "I'll just have to try it. No back-up light on these old tin lizzies. I can't reverse all the way back to the road in the dark."

He did not want the chassis of the car to get stuck between the ruts, so he drove up closer to the edge of the ravine, planning to drive at an angle across them, reverse into the place where the path forked, and then turn the car hood toward the bridge again. This turned out to be a mistake. As he began to reverse, he could feel the back of the car slide to the left instead of turning right in response to the movement of the steering wheel. He cursed, took the car out of reverse, and clambered out. In the reflected light of the headlamps, he saw that the back wheels had slid at least half a meter closer to the edge of the ravine as he turned on the muddy ground.

"Anything I can do?" The voice from the dark interior of the car was still rather tearful.

"Can you drive?" he asked, cool and matter-of-fact.

"Yes, I've . . . a friend of mine sometimes lets me drive her car."

"Right. Get behind the wheel, put her into reverse, and let the clutch in slowly. Go easy on the gas."

The engine roared.

"Less gas!" he shouted, putting all his weight against the left side of the car. But the spinning wheels kept sliding to the left, over the slippery mud. "Stop!" he yelled, breathless. "Bloody hell, didn't I say *less* gas? Let the clutch in *slowly*, I said. Christ, don't *any* women know how to drive?"

"Sorry. I'm not used to this clutch," she said apologetically.

"Now then. Put her into first and go about half a meter forward. And try to *feel* that clutch," he gasped, still breathless.

Once again the engine roared with unnecessary violence, the car slid gently forward . . . and sideways.

"Stop! Now, reverse! And let the clutch in slowly! Keep your foot off the damn gas pedal!"

But it was no better. The wheels spun, and though the young man flung himself against the left side of the car as hard as he could, it still slipped down the gentle slope of the ground toward the edge of the ravine.

"Christ, that was all I needed!" he said, when the engine cut out. He wiped his damp forehead with his shirt-sleeve.

They could hear water splashing at the bottom of the ravine in the silence that had so abruptly taken over from the roar of the engine. The trunks of the sleeping trees merged into the darkness overhead. A spider's web gleamed on a dead branch sticking out from a tree-trunk a few feet away from the car, a regular and perfect web, shining like a miniature neon sign against the depths of the darkness behind it. The spiders are spinning new cobwebs, it'll be a fine day tomorrow, thought the young man. A fine day for whom? Turning his eyes away from the glare of the headlamps, he looked down at the ground. When he got used to the dark, he saw that there was scarcely half a meter between the back wheels and the edge of the ravine.

5

Leaving the lights on, they collected dry branches and put them under the back wheels of the car. The two of them made a strange pair as they moved in silence among the tree-trunks, in the beam of the headlamps. The bearded bandit wiped his face on his shirt-sleeve from time to time, and now and then the slim blonde girl tossed her long hair back over her shoulder, with her own characteristic movement. Her long legs beneath the short black skirt contrasted oddly with the rough bark of the trees. Her shiny black shoes were smeared with yellow mud. The damp chill of past rains rose from the floor of the wood. The girl only had her white blouse, and she was shivering with cold —or with fright? The young man got his jacket out of the car and handed it to his prisoner. "Here, put that on!" He did not help her into it—that would have been going too far—but if he had not been so worried, he would have had to laugh. His jacket was far too big for her, and wearing it she looked as if she had forgotten to put a skirt on. However, he had other things on his mind. He put a lot of branches under the back wheels.

"Now, you stand here and watch the car. See if she goes sideways."

He got in, switched on the engine, and began to reverse, very, very gently. The branches helped, but he could not turn to the right without bringing the front wheels dangerously close to the edge of the ravine. The trouble was that he could not see anything behind him. He stopped again, and got out.

"I think it'll be all right," the girl encouraged him. She was still shivering as if she had a fever, in spite of the jacket.

He was a little surprised. "What's the matter?" he asked. "Hell, look, I'm sorry. I really am. But Christ, I didn't *pick* you, on purpose! It was just Fate or something."

"It's all right," she said. He didn't know if she meant the car or herself.

"Are you still frightened?" he asked gently. "I mean, frightened of me?"

"No," she said quickly.

He bent down to put more dry branches under the back wheels. The pistol in his pocket dug into him as he bent, and he took it out and tossed it in through the car window. Once again he got behind the wheel and drove a little further backwards. That brought the left front wheel closer to the ravine, but it was the only chance of getting on to firmer ground.

However, another reversing maneuver ended with a hollow clang. The chassis of the car had stuck on a muddy piece of rock.

"That's done it!" he said, with assumed cheerfulness. He was at a loss. Looking around him in the darkness that surrounded them like a silent, malicious enemy, he caught sight of the bridge in the reflected light of the headlamps. He went over to the wooden rail and began to tug at the wobbly posts. They creaked. After a while the rusty nails gave way, and he carried the rail back to the car. It was a round pole about fifteen centimeters in diameter, and a good three meters long. "Now for a last attempt," he said, pushing his improvised lever under the side of the car.

He found several of the large stones used to mark the path, and put them under the rail so as to form an effective lever. When he put his weight tentatively on the free end, he could see the left side of the car shift.

"Keep on pushing there till I tell you to stop. Got to get this old cow to see reason somehow."

It was a slow process, but by means of their united efforts they managed to rock the car enough to shift it off the rock.

"Now, you get in and put her in reverse. Go very, very gently. I'll see to the lever."

The girl got into the car, and the old Volkswagen's engine began to tick over hopefully again.

"And mind you *feel* that clutch, or you'll cripple me for life." He realized that if a sudden jerk dislodged his wooden lever and the car slid sideways again, he was going to be crushed against a sturdy hornbeam whose strong roots clung to the edge of the ravine.

As soon as the clutch began to bite, the engine stalled. This happened three times.

"Jesus Christ!" he groaned aloud. The sweat was flowing off him, and he brought all his strength to bear on the lever, but it was no good. "What's the matter with you? Or are you just a hopeless driver? When I

36

say *gently* I don't mean let the engine die! Now, when you feel it's running okay, and the wheels aren't spinning, *then* you can put your foot down, right?"

The engine began to roar, the car moved, leaping backwards with unexpected violence, and then, still roaring and laboring, it made its way across the muddy ruts at an angle, over the path, turning right as it did so, and at last it ended up facing the bridge. The way back to the road lay ahead of them in the beam of the headlamps.

She left the engine running, and got out. But the bandit was nowhere to be seen. She looked around her, puzzled. Then she heard a sound down in the ravine, and after a while a dim, dark shape emerged from the roots of the hornbeam. Slowly and with difficulty, the young man clambered out of the ravine. He was breathing hard, and the girl thought she heard a groan.

"Did—did something happen?" she asked anxiously.

He did not reply, but crawled out of the ravine on hands and knees and sat down on the ground. She saw that he was feeling his right ankle. He rose to his knees, and then tried to stand, but when he was half-way up, he groaned and collapsed on the ground again.

"My fault?" she asked, dismayed.

He said nothing. She could hear his heavy breathing.

"My fault," she said. This time it was not a question.

"No, mine. The whole bloody thing's my fault." He sat there holding his right ankle in both hands, his head resting on his knees. She bent down.

"But what actually happened?"

"Oh, leave me alone!" he groaned. There was nothing but darkness all around them, nothing but darkness as the night ran its course, and the spiders wove new webs for tomorrow. Tomorrow would be a fine day. "Broken, I guess," he said at last. His voice was casual, but there was a wealth of meaning in the words.

She could hear all the things he had left unsaid.

"Here. I'll help you." She took hold of his elbow.

"Get out!" he said. "Go home! Go to hell! I couldn't care less where you go—just get out of here!"

He was sitting with his head on his knees, and she thought he was grinding his teeth. She took his elbow again. "Stand up!" Her voice was cool and authoritative.

He raised his head. "Giving the orders now, are you?"

"I'm not giving any orders. I'm just telling you you'd better get up. I'll help you into the car . . . get you to a doctor."

"The hell with your help! You hear me? The hell with your sympathy. I don't want any sympathy."

He knew it was all over now. With a damaged leg, he didn't stand a chance. Christ, how quickly you could wake from a beautiful dream! Too beautiful, it had been—that was its trouble. Suspiciously beautiful. He could have wept with pain and disappointment, and bitter rage. It was so unfair. Fate was dead against him, every time. Fate? Or had he ruined the whole thing himself?

"I never should have gone thinking about people's feelings," he said bitterly. "To hell with you, I should have thought. That's what I should have done all along. Damn fool!"

In silence, she took his elbow and helped him up. He stood on his left leg, not touching the ground with his right.

"You'd better lean on me," she said.

However, he pushed her away, managing to keep his balance by resting the toes of his right foot lightly on the damp fir twigs. Then he put the foot on the ground. Even in the dim light, she could see an expression of surprise and distrust on his face. He took a limping step, and then a couple more. He still looked distrustful. The ankle must have been sprained, and the dislocated bone had gone back into place when he stood up. It burned, however, as if his whole foot were plunged in boiling water, and his legs were trembling like the legs of a racehorse at the end of a race—but it was not broken! He limped up and down on the wet twigs, feeling slightly ashamed.

They got into the car. The girl sat down, and then felt underneath her in the dark. She produced the pistol, and handed it to him. "Not very comfortable to sit on."

He smiled, awkwardly. He was not sure what to say.

6

However, the episode had not really turned out so well after all. When he first had to put his right foot down on the brake, he groaned with pain. The road was beginning to go downhill, and there were several sharp bends. He pulled in to the side. "Here, you'll have to take over. I can't use my left foot for the clutch *and* the brake—too risky."

So they changed places. She drove very cautiously, for the car lights were not much good now; the old battery, nearly exhausted by the delay in the wood, made them reddish and dim. It was a long time before either he or she said anything, but finally the girl spoke. She had recovered from the shock; she even attempted a joke. "Your turn to get a fright. Makes a change, anyway."

He laughed briefly, but did not reply. There was another pause, a very long one.

"How are you going to manage?" she asked.

"Just what I was wondering myself."

"It's my fault, this happening to you. Listen, I'll take you anywhere you like."

"Anywhere?" he echoed her, with a touch of bitterness. "Hardly!"

"Well, naturally I didn't mean Tahiti!"

"Stop laughing at me, will you? You don't understand."

There was yet another long silence. They could see the lights of houses over to the right, down by the lake whose waters lay there in the dark.

"Did you really mean it? All that stuff about Tahiti?" she asked.

Instead of answering her, he began to think out loud. "Either you're as cunning as they come, and you've been putting on this great act for my benefit—crying like that and all—or else you're bloody well straight. Do you really think I'm going to tell you everything? My whole plan?"

"I didn't mean that. I just wondered, that's why I asked. But I did mean it about driving you anywhere you need to go. One good turn deserves another, and so on. Fair's fair."

"So you think I've been fair to you?"

"In a way."

"Then I can count on you not going to the police till tomorrow morning?"

"Yes. I told you."

"But that'll mean trouble. For you. The police will make things pretty hot for you. I'm just telling you, so you know where you stand. So I know where *I* stand too."

"That's my problem," she said. She was deep in thought.

"Okay, then. Fair's fair."

He felt very nervous as they drove through the little town of Schwyz. He thought he must get rid of the car soon. It was a dead give-away. Reviewing his plan mentally, he wondered how he was going to manage with a bad leg. How would he get his rucksack, containing his clothes, his sleeping bag, his cans of food, up to the barn in the mountains? They were not far from Brunnen now. He'd get rid of his hostage in Brunnen, and he'd get to Erstfeld somehow or other, even if he did have to use the same foot for both clutch and brake. There weren't any really steep gradients on that stretch of road. He must cut his hair and shave before he reached Erstfeld. And he'd change his shirt —and count the money. The Bellinzona express did not leave till after midnight, so he was doing all right for time. He tried to keep his mind on the money lying hidden in the bag on the back seat, and found that he still couldn't. Instead he was thinking about the blonde girl sitting there beside him, driving his old car. Everything seemed slightly unreal, and though there was a huge sum of money on the seat back there, it occurred to him that there might not really be any islands in the South Seas at all, and it was all just a dream, from which he would wake to some other, harsh reality.

Well, reality was harsh all right. When the old Volkswagen stopped outside Brunnen station, there was an embarrassed tension between the two occupants. They both felt that all the usual farewell phrases would sound absurd in this context.

"Can I go now, then?" she asked, breaking the silence.

"Yes. Of course." He tried to sound indifferent, but there was a certain sadness in his voice. "But you've only got your blouse—you can't go off like that! The jacket's no good either. Makes you too conspicuous by half. Hold on—I'll find you something else. I've got a decent raincoat in the trunk. A maxi-coat on you, but you'll pass, if you turn the sleeves up a bit!" He tried to make a joke of it, not very successfully.

He opened the door and got out, but as soon as he put his weight on his right foot he groaned with pain, and if he had not been holding on to the open door he would have fallen. He collapsed back on the seat, wiping his forehead with his shirt-sleeve. He knew he had little real chance of reaching the mountains. The fuzz would get him tomorrow, even if he did shave and cut his hair. A bandit with a limp! Anyone could tell him a mile off! He went pale; he was feeling sick.

The girl was asking him a question, but he did not take it in. He was thinking about her, and how she was the cause of all his bad luck. Yet, funnily enough, he didn't hate her. He just felt sorry it had all turned out so badly. He was overcome by self-pity, and grief for his lost paradise.

"Now what?" asked the girl, after a long time.

Glancing at his face, she realized that there was some savage conflict of feelings going on inside him. This was the first chance she had had to see his face properly, and even the thick beard could not disguise its youth. She saw it all clearly, at close range: the beads of sweat on his forehead, the pale skin stretched taut over his hooked nose, the faint lines in the outer corner of his left eye. Light from the station shone through the windshield, showing it all up.

"I have to get to the mountains. I have to get there somehow," he said, in a strangled voice. He was thinking out loud; he didn't mind her hearing him. He didn't mind anything now, because he thought, in his heart, he would never reach the mountains.

"Whereabouts?" she asked.

He thought there was a note of superiority in her voice, but he did not mind that either; it didn't even annoy him now. He looked away from the station building, at which he had been gazing the whole time without really seeing it, and turned his face toward his hostage—his hostage, who had brought him such bad luck. He, too, was having his first really close look at her. She did not glance away when their eyes met. She repeated her question, and he answered. He told her about the deserted old barn in the mountains above Bellinzona. He told her his plan: how he had meant to stay in his hide-out for a fortnight, or perhaps three or four weeks, until the hue and cry died down a bit, and how he was going to cut his hair, and shave, and about the passport photo. But he did not say anything about Tahiti and the South Seas.

"How far is it? This barn, I mean," she asked, matter-of-fact.

"At least three hours' walk from Bellinzona station. I did it once, to check."

"If I helped you, do you think you could make it?"

He looked steadily at her. He did not know what to think, and she obviously realized his dilemma. "Let's get this clear, shall we?" she said. "That was an awful thing you did, back there, and they'll get you for it sooner or later. But I don't want them to get you because of me, see?"

"Yes."

Hope revived in him as he looked at her face, framed in the long fair hair. It was strange to think that, only an hour ago, he had seen that same face distorted by frightened tears. Frightened of an armed bandit, she'd been! Christ, is this really happening? Or is it that all women need to look after someone? Who does she touch with those long, pretty fingers? Who's allowed to stroke that silky fair hair? He could have dwelt on that subject for much longer, but she was asking whether he would be able to limp up to the barn.

"Look, suppose this ever came out . . . you'd be in one hell of a mess then."

"You leave that to me. Anyway, you have a pistol in your pocket, haven't you?"

"Yes," he said. "Yes . . . that's right. Doesn't work, though. Just a bit of old junk." Christ! So he'd told her that too!

"Well, if you're worried about me and the police, then you didn't tell me that about the pistol, did you?"

"Okay. Look—why are you doing this?"

"I've told you once already. I want them to get you, but not because of me. Anyway . . . I hope you'll think better of it and go to the police with me and give yourself up."

"You're on the wrong track there, lady!" he said, suddenly hostile. "You really think there's anything good about this filthy world? Those bastards in uniform—they run the whole show. It stinks!"

"Now listen; do you or don't you want me to help you?"

"Yes, I do," he said truthfully. And indeed there was nothing in the world he wanted more. "But how am I supposed to believe you'll help a bandit hide out, and then go back and tell the cops in Zürich you don't know where he is?"

"I'll say . . . I'll say you dropped me off in Bellinzona, at the station, and then you went on to Italy," she said, rather uncertainly.

"That'd be disastrous! For you. I don't want you getting into trouble over me."

"*You've* got into trouble over *me*. And now I don't know what to do," she said unhappily. "Can't you trust me? It'll all work out somehow."

"I'll just have to trust you, I suppose," he replied.

The old Volkswagen began to shudder and cough again. Eventually the engine caught, and they drove along the road past the Lake of Lucerne, toward Altdorf.

"I'm glad you told me," she said. "About the pistol."

He did not reply for some time. Then he asked, "What's your name?"

"It doesn't matter," she said evasively. She sounded shy.

After that, they did not talk any more.

7

You could only tell that there was water down there, below the level of the road, when it reflected the lights of houses on the far side. On this side of the lake, the road was cut into the rock, following every twist and turn of the wild, mountainous country. The place was a tourists' paradise. There was one spot, a flat, rocky plateau surrounded by an iron railing, which had an asphalted parking area for motorists who wanted to enjoy the view over the blue-green waters of the Lake of Lucerne, or take a picture for the family photo album. Now, late in the evening, it was deserted, but in spite of that, or perhaps because of it, the old Volkswagen stopped there and stood, its lights switched off, under a pole surmounted by a strong electric light which shone through a faint, conical haze of mist; it looked like an enormous lampshade hanging from the top of the pole. It was quiet and peaceful here, with only the oil spots on the asphalt, which looked dull and black in the artificial light, to remind one of the daytime crowds and bustle.

The bandit climbed out of the car, leaning on the girl. He mastered his pain, stifling a groan, and went to get something from the trunk of the car. Eventually he found it. It was an implement with a razor for cutting hair set into it, such as barbers use. He sat down on the stone wall; the waves were splashing somewhere far below.

"I was going to cut it off to just above my shirt collar," he said.

The girl took the razor from him, and began to cut. Locks of his thick hair fell over the wall in the dark. When she had finished she stepped back to survey her handiwork. The change in his appearance obviously surprised her, and she tood there passing the razor from one hand to the other.

"Give it here!" he said impatiently, taking it from her. "I can do the rest myself."

Peering into a pocket mirror in the bad light, he began to remove his thick, bushy beard, so absorbed in his task that he took no notice of the girl at all. She, however, was rooted to the spot, fascinated by the gradual alteration taking place before her. Seeing the bandit's face change was like watching a butterfly creep slowly out of a chrysalis, not knowing beforehand what shape or color it might turn out to be.

"There," he said after a while, running the razor a few last times over his upper lip. "I'll have a proper shave tomorrow."

He turned his face away from the mirror, looked at the girl, and laughed—his boyish laugh. He looked so amazingly young and boyish that she simply could not get used to it. Her eyes were wide with surprise. It was an extraordinary alteration: like seeing an actor remove a mask.

"How old are you?" she whispered at last.

48

"Twenty," he said quickly, adding a couple of years. He felt rather embarrassed when he saw her surprise. "Look, d'you mind helping me stand up? Got to get rid of this shirt."

Limping over to the car, he fished a plain blue shirt out of the trunk. When he took off the check shirt, his white torso stood out against the dark background. He was thin and angular, not an ounce of fat on him, just skin stretched over his bones and muscles. Not a boy, not quite a man yet. He saw the expression on her face, though he did not know how to interpret it. However, he felt it was not the moment to say anything about the change in his own appearance; it would be beneath him, too! Instead, he asked, "How old are *you* then?"

"Eighteen," she said automatically. However, she seemed to feel this was too intimate and personal a topic of conversation. "Come on, we'd better make a move. I'm getting cold."

They got into the car. The next part of his plan had been to count the money, but he felt awkward about doing that in front of her. In any case, he didn't really want to think about the money. He felt that he was in a strange state of intoxication, where reality mingled with something dream-like. He could not exactly account for it, but he felt it was caused by the girl with the long blonde hair. He wished he could go on feeling like this for a long time. A very long time. For days and days, and never wake up.

Outside Erstfeld station, however, he pulled himself together. "Look, do you realize just how risky this is?" he asked. "If they pick me up before we get on the train, they could say you were acting as my accomplice."

"Oh, and what am I supposed to do? Go off and leave you, when I got you into this mess?"

"No!" he said at once.

"After all, you do have that pistol in your pocket!"

This time he did not laugh. He was thinking hard. "Take off that jacket," he said. "You can wear the raincoat; it's longer. And you could make that scarf around your neck into some kind of turban, and hide your hair under it."

They left the car in the darkness outside the station. He was wearing the imitation-leather jacket now, while she wore his long raincoat. It was of a fashionable skimpy cut, so it did not seem very much too big for her, and the turned-up sleeves were not over-conspicuous. He had the big rucksack on his back, and she was carrying a medium-sized bag. They looked like a couple of young people going away for a weekend together.

Leaning on the girl's left arm, he managed to limp slowly to the platform, where they sat down on a seat. It was an hour before the train would come in, and there was not a soul on the platform, but he felt as though a thousand eyes were watching them. It took him some time to recover from the attack of nerves he had had as they were buying the tickets. As for the girl, she seemed depressed, as if she were thinking of the possible consequences of her action. Here, in the glare of the bright neon lighting, they did not so much as glance at one another.

The hands of the electric clock came around toward midnight. Saturday was ending, Sunday was beginning.

50

"Are you sorry?" he asked, breaking the silence after half an hour. "Sorry you did it?"

"There are a lot of things I'm sorry for," she said cryptically.

He did not ask any more questions, for he felt a vast gap, wide as an ocean, yawning between them on this huge, empty, garishly lit station. It struck him that every human being was really like a shipwrecked sailor on a desert island. He tried to think about the money, now packed among the can of food in his rucksack, but it was no good. He tried to think about the girl sitting beside him, but that was no good either. A strange sense of grief overcame him. In this dismal place, hemmed in by concrete, iron bars, rails, he could not get rid of his old picture of the world: a place full of filth, that's what it was. To start with, there was something ill-defined, but cold and gray. Then the gray walls of the approved school. Then the garage, stinking of oil and gasoline; then the bars—they stank too—full of little tarts. Then a whole crowd of cops, and a beating-up, and a cell with a barred window. A filthy, stinking place. Oh, Christ, the island! he thought. The island in the South Seas, with palm trees and hot sand, warm sea, clouds sailing by, coming from nowhere, going nowhere—and no worries! Probably isn't true. Probably doesn't really exist. You drift on a plank or a barrel or a board or something, and when you do come ashore there's nothing on the island but cold, barren rocks . . .

8

There were not many people on the night express to Italy. They got into an empty compartment, and the young man thought he was in luck after all. Except that there was too much light in the compartment; that bothered him.

They cast surreptitious glances at each other, but that was all. When the inspector came around to see their tickets the young man looked out of the window at the dark countryside with apparent indifference. They were passing through a valley in the mountains; now and then they could see lights in an empty street, or the gleaming water of a river, and the cold, white disc of the full moon sometimes emerged from scraps of flying cloud. The clouds were thinner now. However, when the young man turned and put out his hand to take back the tickets, the girl saw beads of sweat standing out on his damp forehead. She knew he was going to wipe them away, and so he did, the moment the inspector left, with a clean handkerchief taken from the pocket of the sports jacket. The other, dirty handkerchief was wet with her own tears. He smiled rather self-consciously.

"Sweating like a pig. Don't know why. I don't usually sweat at all!"

She knew why he was sweating, just as she knew why this situation was not "usual." She looked at the window—not out of the window; she was gazing at the scene reflected in the glass. Another compartment hovered out there, beside the railway carriage, brightly lit, with two strangers sitting in it. Or were they just illusions? Everything was strange and ghostly. She turned away from the window and looked at the floor. She saw a foot stretched out in front of her, wearing a muddy sandal. The narrow leg of the blue jeans had ridden up, and she could see part of its owner's hairy calf, and his sock, the elasticized top of which had bitten deep into the swelling. Indeed, his leg was so swollen that she could not see his ankle at all.

"You'll have to put cold compresses on that ankle tomorrow," she said quietly.

"Tomorrow? It's tomorrow now," he said, looking at his watch.

That was all the conversation they had during the whole journey.

The express passed through the St. Gotthard tunnel, hurried down the sloping track that ran alongside the river Ticino at the foot of the southern slopes of the Alps, and came into Bellinzona at two thirty.

There were not many passengers getting out so late at night. Apart from the limping bandit and his companion, there were only two elderly married couples, obviously Germans, with a great deal of heavy luggage. They were either on holiday or staying with friends somewhere near Locarno, because there were two cars with Locarno number plates outside the old station building. They were expected. After many loud greetings, and a lot of noise over the luggage, and banging of car doors, both cars drove off.

Leaning on the girl, the young man limped painfully along the deserted street in the pale moonlight. On this side of the Alps, the sky was clear and full of stars. It was a damp, warm night.

When they had crossed the bridge over the river, he dropped the rucksack on the ground and sat down on a milestone by the roadside. He was exhausted by pain. He wiped his face, throat and neck with the handkerchief.

"Is it very bad?" she asked sympathetically.

He did not reply.

"I could carry the rucksack," she said, though doubtfully, since she had scarcely been able to lift it when they got out of the train. "What on earth have you got in there, anyway? It weighs a ton!"

Instead of answering, he bent down, opened the rucksack, and took out a big, thick, leather-bound book, the kind you only see in second-hand shops these days. He raised it and threw; the book shot into the undergrowth. He took out another book, only slightly smaller than the first, and threw that away too. Stooping for the third book, he inadvertently put his weight on his bad leg, and dropped the book.

The girl picked it up and handed it to him.

"Just pornography," he said, flinging it away.

But she had had time to see the title as it lay on the ground. *Across the Pacific Ocean.*

"Dirty pictures and so on. I was going to pass the time with it, up there."

He had bought the old travel books ages ago out of
his wages, when he was an apprentice. He was ashamed
of them. He loved old books about distant lands, and
he had read these several times, from cover to cover.
Travel books gave him a wonderful sense of release.
However, he was as ashamed of reading them as of
masturbation.

"Why do you have to make everything out worse
than it really is?" she asked.

"How do you mean, everything?"

"You want me to think you're no good at all, don't
you?"

"Well, aren't I?"

She did not know what to say.

"The hell with that, anyway. I can't throw away the
cans, but we've got to get clear of this damn road before morning, whatever happens."

She helped him hoist the rucksack on his back. At
least it was a bit lighter now.

However, they made very slow progress. He had to
stop and rest very frequently. Then they heard the
distant sound of a heavy motor vehicle breaking the
silence of the night, and after a while the asphalt took
on a yellowish tinge, and long shadows leaped into life
ahead of them. A heavy truck was coming up behind.
It slowed down as it passed, and stopped a little way
in front of them. The driver put his head out of the
cab window.

"*Cosa c'è?*" he asked in Italian.

"He wants to know what's happened," said the girl.

"Tell him we're on a holiday, walking in the mountains, and I've hurt my leg."

They went up to the truck. It was a ten-tonner, with
a tarpaulin over it.

"Say I slipped on a rock."

"What happened?" the driver asked again, in bad German this time.

"We're on a holiday," said the young man. "Walking. I slipped off a rock—sprained my ankle."

"I give you a lift," said the driver in German. He was a young man, with dark, wavy hair which, as they could see in the light of the full moon, was wet and recently combed. He added in Italian, looking at the girl, "I'm going to Gordola to pick up my mate. I can take you along."

"What did he say?" asked the young man.

"He said he'd give us a lift."

The diesal engine was purring softly.

"Mountains good for goats," said the driver, in German. "For people, music better, dancing better— *vero?* Mountains, foot get hurt. Music *bene.*" He began to laugh.

Opening the door of the cab, he helped the young man up with his rucksack.

The truck drove slowly off; the girl was sitting between the driver and the bandit.

"Sunday I work!" said the driver cheerfully. "More cash—you know? More cash! Whole world, need more cash. You know?"

"Sure, I know," said the youth, with a forced laugh. He knew all right.

The girl was looking melancholy.

"Signorina sad. I back this afternoon. Go dancing this evening. Signorina come? Him at home—bad leg. I, no bad leg." He persevered for some time in trying to start a conversation, but without success. He gave up, but he did not lose his good humor; he began to sing to himself above the noise of the engine.

The young man looked out of the cab window at the moonlit countryside. They drove through a cluster of houses. As they reached the last one, he suddenly said, "Stop, please! This is it. We're on holiday here—staying with friends. That's our car, that white one."

The driver leaned forward to look out of the right-hand window. There was a white car outside the garage of an obviously new villa, standing in the garden.

"Ford Mustang," he said. *"Bene*—but hungry like elephant, that car."

When the young man and the girl had climbed out, the driver leaned out of the open door and called, in Italian, "Sure you won't come dancing this evening, signorina? I'll pick you up in my car, okay?"

"Sorry! My husband wouldn't like it!" she said, laughing to soften the refusal.

"Okay, then, if that's your husband—same as that's your car!" He laughed. "It's got a local number plate, though. I'll come around anyway, just in case! Six o'clock, right?" He closed the door and drove off.

"What was he saying?" asked the young man, when he had settled the rucksack on his back. He was leaning on the girl's right arm.

"Asking if I'd go dancing with him."

"What did you say?"

"I said no. Then he said he'd come around at six all the same."

"Bastard. Let's hope he's cooled off by then. Let's hope he doesn't read the papers or listen to the radio."

About half an hour later they reached a little bridge over a mountain stream, and a narrow, stony path which led uphill along the bank of the stream.

"It's about two hours' walk from here. In the normal way," he said gloomily, looking up at the stars. Above the eastern horizon the blue-black sky was beginning to pale and take on a tinge of green. "Better get a move on. It'll soon be light."

The stony path was uneven where heavy rain had made ruts in it; it was much worse than walking along the road. They had to stop and rest every twenty meters or so, and all the time the young man was finding it harder. He stumbled over a stone and nearly fell where the path vanished into the shadow of the trees. When they stopped in a little moonlit copse, the girl saw tears on her companion's face, though he was not crying.

"Does it hurt a lot?" she asked anxiously.

"It bloody does," he said, swallowing hard.

"Are you angry with me?"

"Angry with you? No. No, I'm sorry about you. I've got you into a right mess, I know that. You're in real trouble, just for helping someone like me. The fuzz don't forget that sort of thing in a hurry."

"It's my own fault."

"Yes, the same as me ever being born is your fault! I can tell you, some people come into the world just to make trouble—for themselves and other people!" He sounded about eighty years old. He was sitting on the rucksack, and his pale face in the moonlight looked as if it were made of marble.

She stole another glance at him; she still had not got over the change in his appearance. She helped him to stand up and hoist the rucksack on his shoulders.

They walked slowly on for almost an hour, but then the pain won and the bandit gave up. He rubbed the sweat out of his eyes. "I'll never make it. It's getting light. Suppose someone meets us . . ." In a moment or so he recovered a little, and went on, "I know. I'll spend the day somewhere in the bushes, by the stream here. And make cold compresses for my ankle. Then I'll go on in the evening. I'll get up there if I have to crawl on my hands and knees! You go home now. They'll be waiting to hear from you."

"There's no one waiting to hear from me."

Taken aback, he looked at her face, framed in golden hair again, for she had removed the scarf as soon as they turned off the road and started up the mountain path. Her sleepless night had left her with dark rings under her eyes. In the hazy, gentle light of dawn, against the dark background of the wooded slope, she looked like a Madonna in a painting by some old master. The young man had not been into many museums or churches, but he did remember a Madonna which one of his mates at the garage had pinned up in his clothes locker, years ago, a reproduction of some old painting. His friend, a pious lad, had stuck three color pictures of nudes from *Quick* magazine up under it.

"There's no one waiting to hear from me at home," she repeated.

"You've got parents, haven't you? And a home somewhere?"

"I've got parents. Not a home. I ran away from home."

"When?"

"A week ago."

"What for?"

"I don't know."

"But you must have had a reason."

"Not any particular reason. That's the trouble."

He wanted to ask where she was living now, but it struck him that she might be living with some man. He did not like the idea.

"Well, yes, I did have a nice home. They're pretty well off," she said hesitantly, as if she were telling him some secret which was preying on her mind. "Only I didn't tell you, because I thought you might make a ransom demand."

He ignored this remark. "Why did you leave, then?"

"I just did."

He couldn't make this out. He knew very little about nice homes, where people were pretty well off. All he had known was Uncle Paul's kitchen, the orphanage and the approved school.

"I've been staying with a girl friend this week . . . at least, she isn't really a friend of mine. We don't have anything much in common. And I don't want a man—a man wouldn't think of anything but getting me into bed with him."

"You've got problems, haven't you?" Suddenly he felt a lot better. He was tremendously relieved. Then he realized that they were not, after all, on a holiday together; he was sitting on a rucksack full of stolen money. "Look, you've got to get back home just as fast as you can. On account of the police."

"Yes, I know," she said. "But I feel so tired. I don't mind about anything just now."

Sitting there on the rucksack, he stared at the gravel which the rain had washed down the mountain-side.

"What's your name?" he asked in a low voice. "Your Christian name, I mean."

She did not answer at once, but eventually she replied, "Judith."

9

There was a copse of beech trees to the right of the stony path; behind it rose steep rocks, with a few straggling bushes clinging to them. Over hundreds of thousands of years, a narrow ravine had been cut into the rock at this point, and when the spring thaw came, turbulent muddy water cascaded and tumbled down through the ravine to the valley. But now there was nothing but a little stream of crystal clear water trickling along the bottom. It flowed into a pool at the foot of the rocks. Not a very large pool; a few rocks stuck up out of it, and the flotsam and jetsam of twigs and roots, bleached in the sun, which had come floating downstream idled on the surface. The thick green foliage of the beeches, oaks and elms around the pool, and the dense undergrowth of hazel bushes, hid the place from sight. As the little ravine faced south-east, the sun shone in on the pool at eight in the morning.

When they could go no further, they retreated to the shelter of this pool. He collapsed on to a rock, heaving the rucksack off his back. He removed his sandal and pulled off his sock. The swelling extended from the sole of his foot right over his ankle and half-way up his calf.

"Won't you give up now?" she asked. "Give up the whole idea?"

She saw a cold and unfriendly gleam in his eyes. Now that it was bright daylight, she could see that he had very thick, pointed eyebrows. This, and his hooked nose, gave him a slightly hawk-like appearance.

"You may need a doctor," she said. "It could be broken, after all. I don't want you to end up a cripple because of me. If you . . ."

He interrupted her. "A cripple, okay. But I'm not giving up."

She took his handkerchief, dipped it in the icy water of the pool, and laid it over the swelling. Then she tied the ankle up with her scarf.

"Don't worry," he said softly. Bending over the rucksack, he took out a carefully folded sleeping bag. "Here. It's zipped up. If you unzip it and open it out it'll do for a blanket. Lie down and get some rest."

She obeyed. She spread the sleeping bag out on the ground and lay down; in fact, she was so tired that she could have slept on her feet.

The sun was beginning to shine in on the pool, and the surrounding rocks gave out a comfortable warmth. There was a pleasant smell of water, and the murmur of the stream was soothing. He closed his eyes, leaning back against the rock, so tired that he was quite unable to get his confused thoughts into any kind of order. They went around and around inside his head. If he closed his eyes he felt as if he were in a dream. He opened them a little. The girl was there, lying on the ground at his feet, still wearing his long raincoat, which now covered her from her chin right down to her muddy shoes. But her hair shone in the sunlight as if it were made of gold thread. He shut his eyes once more. He wanted to think, but somehow he couldn't. The cold compress relieved the pain of his foot, and he drifted into a doze and then fell fast asleep.

He was awakened by a stiff neck. At first, he couldn't remember where he was, but then he opened his eyes and saw the figure wrapped in his coat, and knew it was not a dream. He glanced at his watch. He had slept for over an hour and a half. It was time to change the compress on his ankle, but he did not want to wake the sleeping girl. He reached for a dead branch lying just beyond the rock, tied the handkerchief to the end of it, dipped it in the pool, and then bound up his ankle again.

It was getting hot in the little ravine. He took off his jacket, folded it, and put it under his head. Once again he closed his eyes and tried, unsuccessfully, to think of the money. He fell asleep, and had a dream about the picture of a saint hanging up in a dirty garage.

About an hour later the pain in his ankle woke him. He wrapped the handkerchief around the end of the branch and dipped it in the cold water again.

It was hot under the sunlit rocks, and the air above them was quivering in a heat haze. A clump of ferns grew out of a cleft in the rock above the little pool. The tip of one fern frond touched the stream flowing down between the rocks from time to time. The fern floated in a constant circular movement, because as soon as the tip of the frond touched the water, the current tried to carry it on. He watched this strange piece of natural engineering, fascinated, and at the same time he realized he was very thirsty. But he did not want to disturb the peace of this moment. He didn't really want to do anything at all. Just sleep. Sleep, and dream.

Another sound intruded into the monotonous murmur of the water. It roused him; he opened his eyes slightly and listened, but he could not identify it. He sat up. He saw the girl still lying in the same position, and thought she was asleep, but then he noticed her fair head shaking, and realized what the sound was. She was crying, but this time her tears were different: soft, like autumn rain. This was what he'd expected; this was what he'd been afraid of! He had known it was bound to happen. It struck him forcibly that he ought not to be thinking of anything just now except saving his own skin—the same as everyone else. He'd better put his mind to getting out of this trap. Instead, he slid off the rock where he was sitting, supporting himself on his hands, and then, with both hands on the ground behind him, painfully hauled himself over the gravel until he was beside her.

"I knew it! I knew it would be like this!" he said accusingly. "You should have cleared off, right at the start. You should have run away! I'm a bloody fool— should have had more sense myself, right at the start! Can't think what came over me." He wanted to say something else, but he didn't know how; he was at a loss for the right words.

The water murmured on as the minutes passed by.

"Here, are you hungry? Or thirsty?" Though he knew she had had nothing to eat since the afternoon of the previous day, he suddenly felt that this was the wrong moment to ask.

She did not move, but he heard her whisper something through her quiet tears. He could not catch it, because of the sound of the water. He bent his head lower.

"Everything's so awful!" she whispered, through her sobs.

"Why didn't you run away at the start? Hell, I gave you the chance, didn't I? So why . . . ?"

"I don't know. Anyway, everything was awful before. All the time. It was hopeless. And always the same . . ."

"Yes, so now it's different, and even worse!" he said. She went on crying quietly.

"But you can go!" he said, wondering just how he was going to manage. Damn his foot! "You can go now."

"I'd have to tell them. I'd have to tell them everything. I don't *want* to help them . . . don't want to go to prison either."

"Oh, don't you worry about prison," he said bitterly. "You can say I made you do it. Tell them I went to Italy—Milan."

An idea struck her. "Suppose we went together . . ."

"Went where?" he asked, not understanding her.

"Went to the police together, and gave back the money. Then everything would be all right, and . . ."

"Like hell it'd be all right!" he interrupted. The cold, unyielding sensation came over him again. "They'd get me behind bars, that's all. At the speed of light. Anyway, I'm not giving myself up. Not for anything." He was silent for a moment, and then added quietly, "I need that money. I really need it. I don't suppose you understand."

"Yes, I do. I'd like to go somewhere far away, too. But not like this."

"So what are you going to do now?" How different it would have been, he thought, if only she'd run away yesterday evening in that field. So much simpler! He would never have hurt his ankle, there'd be no complications. Yet he was not sure that he really wished it had been that way.

"I just don't know *what* to do," she said helplessly. "I'm frightened."

"What of?"

"Don't know."

He crawled back to the rucksack, rummaged inside it and found a can of liver pâté and a packet of crackers. He opened the can, put the crackers down on a flat stone, and began to spread pâté on them. "Get some food inside you, for God's sake," he told her.

Obediently, she took one of the crackers and ate it. They drank water from the stream, mixed in a mug with a little canned lemon juice. Some ants came crawling over the stone and carried the cracker crumbs away. It was midday.

After their modest midday meal, he took another can out of the rucksack and weighed it thoughtfully in his hand for some time before opening it.

"Pineapple from Hawaii. Didn't know who'd be eating it when I bought it. I thought I'd open it to . . . to celebrate. I like pineapple a lot."

He handed her the can and a small picnic fork.

"But I haven't got anything to celebrate," she protested dismally.

"Getting away. Miraculous escape from the clutches of a bandit . . . Judith."

She glanced up, startled at being addressed by her name.

"Judith," he repeated, as if he enjoyed lingering

over the name more than he enjoyed the taste of the pineapple. "Can I ask you a question?"

She waited to hear what it was.

"This is a purely theoretical question, see? Suppose I did go to the police. Do you think we might see each other again, some time? It's a purely theoretical question."

"Yes. I think so. That's a purely theoretical answer."

His face darkened. He could have kicked himself. You fool, he thought, you goddam fool! What's the matter with you, shooting your mouth off like this? Thinking of throwing it all up for some silly little girl, are you? Some bored little bitch with plutocratic morons for parents! She's out to get you, chum, with her Madonna face, and don't you forget it. It's you she's after. Wants to take you home to Mummy and Daddy and say, hey, look what I've found myself! So then they sit you down at a table in front of a great big plate of stuffed turkey, or whatever these rich morons eat. And then they ask, all polite and respectful: Where did you do your engineering studies? And you say: At the approved school in Dortmund. Oh yes, and I did the practical part of the course in a stinking garage, flat on my back in the oil on a cold concrete floor. So then dear rich Daddy says: Splendid! And dear plump Mummy says: Be good to our little Judith, won't you?

"What's the matter? You look terrible," said Judith. "Is your ankle hurting?"

"I just remembered the cops," he said. "The fuzz. The bastards. Hell, of course I'm not going to the police!"

She was silent for a moment or so. "Nor me," she said. "Not today."

10

They lay side by side on the improvised blanket all afternoon. The June sun beat down on the rocks here on the southern slopes of the mountains. The murmuring water, the warmth and the quiet lulled them asleep; they slept, and woke, and slept again. Once, when the young man woke and heard the girl breathing deeply and peacefully, he thought that now, at last, he could count the money. He still had no idea how much it was. He crept quietly over to the rucksack, but instead of counting the money he took out his razor, hauled himself over to the pond, and had a proper shave. Then he lay down again and dozed off. He was not worrying about anything at the moment. He told himself it was up to Fate, everything would solve itself somehow or other, he was still young, things were bound to turn out all right.

As the afternoon wore on, the shadow of the rocks fell over the ravine, and it turned cool. They nibbled sweet biscuits and drank lemon and water. She noticed that he had shaved.

"Why, when there's no one up here?" she asked.

"How do you mean, no one? There's a lady up here,

right? Anyway, *I* always heard that a real gentleman shaves even when he's on his own!"

She laughed for the first time since yesterday evening. She was rested now, and she too was beginning to think that it was all Fate, and she was young, and it might yet end well.

"What made you laugh, then? The first thing I said, or the second?"

"Both!" she replied, and he joined delightedly in her laughter. After all, he thought, he did have a number of reasons to feel cheerful, including the fact that all the cold compresses had made the swelling on his ankle go down a bit.

When evening came the moon rose, hanging low over the horizon, incredibly large. An orange moon, like a Japanese lantern. The young man was ready to start, his rucksack on his back. He hoped walking would be easier now, for before dark, quite by chance, he had found a slender, fallen beech sapling, which gave him the idea of making himself a crutch. The sapling had two main branches, which he had trimmed away with his pocket knife, with some difficulty, and the remaining stumps formed the fork of a crutch. He fitted it under his arm, and they set off.

Judith was wearing the long coat again, its sleeves turned up, for there was a cool breeze blowing from the evening sky. However, in spite of the crutch they were not going any faster than before. The pain in his ankle was unbearable, and after half an hour he found that the crutch was chafing the skin of his armpit. He took his shirt out of the rucksack and wrapped it around the fork of the crutch, but by now his armpit was so sore that he could not rest any weight on it. He was also getting a cramp in his right hand, the hand that gripped the crutch. He groaned and clenched his teeth together, wiped the sweat from his face and went on. Now and then the girl stole a glance at his face, but she dared not say anything. She was contrite, seeing him in pain and feeling it was all her fault. And observing the dogged determination with which he overcame his pain, she knew she could hardly hope that this obstinate young man would give himself up of his own free will.

They sat down on the trunk of a fallen tree. Somewhere, far below, lights were switched on in thousands of homes, but up here it was an entirely different world. A world with only two people in it. Pain and effort were tormenting the young man, but they were not in the forefront of his mind; they were minor details, automatically present, like breathing. He could not take his mind off the girl, Judith, not for a second. It was like being ill. Mentally, he cursed himself. He wondered how it would be if the money were not there in the rucksack at his feet. To hell with the money. If he were not a criminal and an outlaw. If he'd never had this bloody idea at all. Only, if he had *not* had the idea, and if he were *not* a criminal, then the girl called Judith would not be sitting there beside him. So he tried to think about something quite different. He imagined himself on board a ship, leaning on the rail and looking out at the sea in the clear light of a tropical moon, with Judith leaning against him. A cool wind blew off the sea, mingled with salty spray, and Judith shivered. He took off his coat and put it around her shoulders. She smiled at him and freed her hair from the coat collar with her own characteristic gesture, tossing it back behind her. The gentle breeze seized her long hair and blew it in his face . . . The white sand was hot, even in the shade of the palm trees leaning over the emerald-green waters of the little bay, and if you stretched out on your back all you could see was the tops of the palms and the white clouds above them. The place was wonderfully peaceful, for the island was completely deserted. Then the tree-tops disappeared, and so did the clouds, and there was a face there, framed in golden hair. Close to his own face he saw two eyes, and the whole world mirrored in them. He lifted his hand and touched this face with his fingertips, just to convince himself it was really there, and Judith whispered: What is it? What are you thinking . . . ?

"How much further?" Judith asked, out loud.

II

They reached the barn just after eleven. The moon was white now, and high in the sky, casting its dim light, drawn from somewhere on the other side of the world, over the low building of rough, irregular stones. The moonlight was cold and dead, unable to give the old walls even the illusion of life; the whole place looked dead and stony. Even the roof was made of stone, with flat, irregular slabs of granite laid over the beams like tiles. There were two small, unglazed windows in the stone walls, looking like yawning black holes with emptiness behind them, and the heavy, dilapidated wooden door hung on one hinge. It was open, and the dark gap between door and wall looked gloomy and menacing.

He felt he ought to say something cheerful. He stood leaning on his crutch, breathing hard.

"It's not so bad in the daytime. Gets a lot of sun."

He slipped the rucksack off his shoulders, dropped it in the grass and sat down on it, bending over his right ankle to turn up the trouser leg. His leg was badly swollen again, right up to his calf.

"Is there any water here?" she asked anxiously. She felt afraid of the place—the dead light on the stones, the door hanging from its hinges, the two menacing black holes, the general air of desolation about it.

"Around the other side," he said. "There's a stone water trough there, and an iron pipe sticking out of the hillside. There's always water trickling out of it—good water, too. A mineral spring, I shouldn't be surprised. These mountains are full of mineral springs." He felt he had to cheer her up somehow. "When I was up here a month back . . ." Suddenly he stopped dead, turned his head and listened. The moon shone on his face, which was pale as marble, and when he turned his head to one side his hawk nose was outlined against the dark shadow of the barn. "Christ, that'd be just my luck! Just about all I needed! One hell of a complication, that'd be."

She had no idea what he meant.

He told her. When he was last here, the water had been flowing from the pipe into the trough all the time . . . so why couldn't they hear it now? He tried to stand up, but after the long climb his ankle was in such a bad way that even with the help of the crutch he could not rise to his feet.

"Judith, please, will you go and look? It *can't* have dried up, not in June!"

She obeyed, though reluctantly, for the other side of the barn was in shadow, and she was much more frightened of the dark than of the bandit. He seemed to realize how she felt, for though he drew in his breath sharply with pain, he managed to rise, leaning on the crutch, and limp along behind her.

There was a tin can standing on the edge of the stone trough, just below the end of the rusty pipe. Water was flowing out of the pipe, into the can, and then down the side of it and thus into the trough. That explained why they had not heard the usual trickling sound on the other side of the barn. He looked at the can in silence. So the place was not quite as deserted as he had thought. Who could have left the can here? A tourist? Not very likely. He noticed dog's pawmarks in the mud below the trough. Maybe some shepherd came here to drink. There were broad, grassy slopes on the mountain-side above the barn; yes, someone might well be pasturing sheep near by. However, he kept his worries to himself, and pretended to be relieved. "Marvelous water, this—bloody marvelous."

She seemed to have something on her mind, and he felt impelled to keep talking. "Over there—just a bit further down, see?—there's the foundations of a building. Must have burned down a long time ago."

"Who would have put that can here?" asked Judith.

"Oh, just some tourist." He limped back to his rucksack and produced a flashlight from one of its side pockets.

The door groaned shrilly as he slowly opened it, swinging on its hinges. The girl reached instinctively for his elbow. It all felt uncanny, like a crime play on television, only this was real. Inside the barn, there was a hard mud floor, and several planks and pieces of wood lay heaped up against one wall. There was a decrepit old barrel in one corner, and a big pile of hay on the other side of the barn. The place smelled of mildew and dusty hay. Two small, bright carpets of moonlight lay on the floor; they were the only ornaments in the place.

"You're not going to *live* here, are you?" she asked. Her throat felt tight, and she did not let go of his elbow.

He laughed, briefly. "Live here? No, I'm not going to live here. This is just a kind of a prologue to living— know what I mean? That's all everything's been till now, just one long, goddam prologue." He thought of the sand again, and the swaying palm trees, and the face framed in golden hair, but now he realized how very far away the island was. Judith, Judith . . . He felt her hand on his elbow. He was intensely conscious of her touch, but he knew this was only for today, for now, just for a moment. Tomorrow Judith too would be very far away.

While he sorted out bits of wood to make some kind of a seat, she went to soak the handkerchief in the stone trough. Then they ate their supper, sitting on a plank and spearing pieces of cold corned beef with their only fork, and crunching hard biscuits. He tried to think of something to say to make her smile.

"You know why some people call canned stuff like this the food of the gods? Because God only knows what's in it!"

Even this, however, failed to cheer her up. She said, "I can't help wondering. Wondering where it went wrong."

"Wondering where what went wrong?"

"I mean, which of us made the real mistake?"

Dear Jesus, he thought, you did! "I did," he said.

"Yes, but I mean, where did it *really* start? All the same, you know, I keep thinking it'll turn out all right somehow."

"Don't go thinking like that. I don't," he said, untruthfully. "If you ask me, it's a big mistake to go having attacks of conscience and so forth. Going in for feelings, and all that," he added, still lying in his teeth. "Know what I mean? For instance . . . suppose you have two people, and they meet, and they say they're in love and hop into bed, and—well, they have all those feelings and that. So then they part. They each meet someone else, and hop into bed again, or maybe they do it on a park bench instead, and call *that* love too. More feelings! Then they part too, and so it goes on. Makes you want to throw up, doesn't it?"

He stared at the moonlit mud floor. The dust on the floor looked like sand . . . a sandy beach in an emerald-green bay, hot in the sun, heavy palm fronds swaying above the water. You lie there full length in the lovely peaceful warmth. Like heaven. Only what good is the lovely warmth and the white sand and the emerald-green bay, and the palms and all, if you're on your own with the sand and water and trees? Nothing to touch.

"And people who actually *believe* in all those emotional feelings and that," he said harshly, "well, that's just about the end! I'd rather be alone, thanks very much!"

"Well, you will be tomorrow."

"I didn't mean it that way."

"How did you mean it, then?"

"I meant life gets complicated if you go around believing things. Trusting people. I don't trust anyone. I only trust myself." He was trying to remember things he'd read in magazine stories. Resourceful, worldly-wise, much traveled characters who could stand any idea on its head. He could only remember vague bits and pieces of all sorts of things he had read. "A human being is ninety per cent fluids," he quoted, inappropiately. "The heart is a piece of hard muscle."

"You didn't get that out of your own head!" she said, laughing a little for the first time that evening.

76

"No. Read it in some medical book."

"Do you do a lot of reading?"

"No. No, I bloody don't. Any fool who wants to bare his heart to the public goes and writes a book. Who's going to read all that stuff, then? I'd rather not read at all."

"You make everything out worse than it ıs! Including yourself!"

He laughed, because he did not know what to say to that. When she fell silent, he sat there as if his attention was somewhere far away. At last he said, "Look, you must be worn out after this trip. You'd better get some sleep. I want you to start early in the morning, in case you meet anyone near here."

He put the sleeping bag out for her, and limped outside the barn. When he came back a little later, all that was visible of her was her golden head sticking out of the bag. He knew she was not asleep, but he could not think of anything appropriate to say. He felt depressed, which annoyed him. He was used to feeling angry with himself, but this time he simply felt depressed. He put on his pullover, picked up the raincoat, which was still warm from her body, lay down on the hay and spread it over him.

"Good night, Judith," he said quietly, after some time.

She did not reply, and he thought she must be asleep after all. However, then she spoke, equally quietly. "A gentleman usually tells a lady his name when he addresses her!"

"Oh, Jesus!" he said. "I've got no manners at all, didn't you know? My name's Peter."

He waited for her to say something else, but she remained silent. So he turned on his side, pushed some

of the hay away so that it would not press on his
swollen leg, and tried to go to sleep. He could hear the
loud pulsing of his heart in the dry hay just beneath his
ear.

12

Next morning it was raining. The rain had begun during the night, and by dawn it was heavy, and showed no signs of slackening off. Dim light filtered into the barn through the narrow window, but it could not drive out all the shadows. Thick mist drifted in from outside, clinging to the stone walls, condensing and then trickling down them. Outside the barn there was a smell of wet grass.

Inside the barn, there was a smell of coffee. The small solid spirit stove made creaking noises as it cooled.

They sat on a worm-eaten plank and ate their breakfast. Judith drank her coffee from the mug, Peter from the tin can he had found in the stone trough. The can had held orange juice, and it could not have been there very long, for it was still bright and silvery inside. Who could have left it there? And when?

"You can't go till it clears," he said. "You can have the raincoat anyway, of course, but you can't start out in rain like this."

She was not cheerful company; obviously she was one of those people who find it difficult to wake up and face the world in the morning, and the dismal gray light and cold rain outside did not improve matters. Her long golden hair hung limp on either side of her face. The air was damp, and she had nothing to tidy it with but the half of a comb he had lent her. It was a bandit's comb, greasy, with gaps where it had lost teeth.

"No, I must go. The sooner the better. You said so yourself—rain never hurt anyone."

"Rain didn't. Pneumonia did," he said, concerned.

About ten o'clock, the dull gray sky became a little brighter, and the rain turned to a soft, fine drizzle. She got ready to start.

"It'll only take you an hour and a half to get down."

"Yes."

"The minute you get to the station, have some hot lemon tea. And when you get back to Zürich, tell them I went on to Italy."

"Yes," she said mechanically, as if she were thinking of something quite different.

"If they ask you where you were all Sunday, tell them you don't know. You could say I made you take a pill or something. Sounds a bit crazy, I know, but you have to play it right or you'll land yourself in trouble. Make out you're suffering from shock, okay?"

"Yes."

"Listen, this is life or death for me, Judith. Please."

"Come with me!" she said, suddenly and urgently.

"Oh, for God's sake!" he said angrily. Then he pushed a crumpled note into her hand, for her ticket. She flinched as if she had touched something slimy.

"It's not stolen!" he cried. "That's my own money—
I earned it. I'm not a thief! But you don't understand,
do you?" His words were tumbling over one another.
He really wanted her to go away as quickly as possible,
so he could have some peace and quiet. Christ, things
were difficult enough already, why go in for more complications? She belongs in another world, he thought,
she must go. He wanted to be alone. When he was alone
he was in control of his thoughts, of the world he had
invented for himself, where there was no place for her.
He just wished she would hurry up and go. Or did he?

He limped to the door with her. His foot hurt. He
leaned against the damp stone wall and wondered how
she would say goodbye. She held out her hand; it was
hot.

"Goodbye. And good luck, Peter!" It was the first
time she had called him by his name.

He tried to smile, but could only manage a grimace.
"Well, thanks! You started off wanting them to pick
me up as soon as possible! I really appreciate that!"

She tried to smile too. "You know, you didn't tell me
the truth yesterday," she said, with false cheerfulness.
"You said you didn't trust anyone. You trust me.
Otherwise you wouldn't be letting me go home."

He was still searching for words when she turned
and went away.

He stood there by the door that hung from its
hinges, his back to the damp wall, the improvised
crutch in his hand, and watched her go.

If she turns around, he told himself, then we'll meet
again. He saw her getting smaller and smaller as she
disappeared into the wet mist. She had not turned
around. She was gone, like a mirage. Gone for good.

He went back inside. Now, at last, he would count the money lying under the cans of food in his rucksack! The rucksack lay there, silent and demanding. He went up to it and poked it angrily with his crutch. Then he limped over to the sleeping bag on the bed of hay and put his hand inside it. The quilted wadding was still warm. Not a mirage, then. Taking off his shoes, he crawled into the sleeping bag, closed his eyes, and listened to the water trickling into the stone trough outside.

Part Two

13

When she got to the road she wiped her dirty shoes on a tuft of grass. The wet, black patent shone like new, but their toes and sides were scratched by the stones. They were fashionable shoes with square toes and broad, medium-height heels, not intended for a world of mud and stones. They came from the Bahnhofstrasse, where they had cost sixty francs, and now, scarred by stones and deformed by the rain, they were on their way back to the world where they belonged.

The wet asphalt of the road smelled of rain even though the rain had stopped now. Heavy vehicles sped by, raising clouds of spray. She walked on the left of the highway, avoiding puddles, even though her shoes were ruined already. She walked slowly; her calf muscles were stiff after the long, steep climb down, and the little toe of her right foot hurt at every step where the wet shoe squeezed it.

The white car was still standing outside the garage of the new villa, though it was facing away from the road today. A mascot lay on the shelf behind the rear window, a big, furry, orange-and-black striped tiger . . . That's our car, that white one . . . on a holiday here, staying with friends . . . Mustang *bene,* but hungry like elephant . . . In the daylight, she could see that the car had a big scratch all along its left side. The lucky tiger mascot had wild, yellowish-black eyes.

Cars rushed by, their tires swishing. It was Monday morning, and everyone was in a hurry. No one stopped. Judith looked like a hippie in the long raincoat, and her damp hair tucked under the scarf. Drivers in a hurry don't stop for hippies.

She walked slowly toward the station, moving like a robot. First she bought a ticket to Zürich, then she went to look at the timetable and find out the time of the next train. She felt wearier than she had ever been in her life before. Her brain refused to function; she stared at the letters and numbers indicating times of arrival and departure without taking them in. It was a cool, gray, ordinary day.

She went into the buffet and bought a packet of cigarettes, a box of matches and a cup of hot lemon tea . . . The minute you get to the station have some hot lemon tea . . . when you get back to Zürich tell them I went on to Italy . . . you have to play it right . . . suffering from shock . . . life or death . . . She was sitting alone at a small square table. A glass and an orangeade bottle with some dregs left in it still stood there. She lit a cigarette and took alternate gulps of warm smoke and hot, bitter tea. She liked coffee better than tea. Why hadn't she bought herself coffee? She'd never liked lemon tea, ever since she was a child. An old woman in a blue overall removed the glass and the orangeade bottle and wiped the shiny red surface of the table with a damp cloth.

There were two men drinking beer at the next table,

discussing Sunday's football games loudly in Italian. A truck came to a halt outside the buffet; she could hear metal containers banging about and the jangle of bottles. It was Monday morning.

She smoked her cigarette and took small sips of the hot lemon tea she had never liked. It was sour and bitter, but she drank it down to the last drop. The little toe of her right foot was sore and burning, as if she had rubbed salt into an open wound. Every time she moved coins jingled in her coat pocket . . . It's not stolen . . . you don't understand . . . The tea was revolting, the cigarette left her with an unpleasant taste in her mouth, and her wet feet were chilly in their sodden shoes; the floor was draughty.

She got up from the table and went in search of a telephone booth, limping slightly. She knew what she wanted: she wanted to get back in touch with a world where there were no chilly draughts, a warm, dry world where there was safety and security and no one was hungry.

The old gray stones of the platform had been worn by millions of feet. The paint on the *art nouveau* cast-iron pillars and the vaulting supporting the roof above the tracks had turned yellowish and black, and the smell of carbolic rose from the wooden sleepers, covered with rusty dust. The only bright, new thing in sight was a row of phone booths up against the wall near the way out of the old station building. Inside, however, they smelled of stale cigarette smoke. She dialed the Zürich code, then her home telephone number, but before the connection was made she hung up and dialed another number instead. Her father's office number.

"It's me. Judith," she said quietly, when a man's voice answered.

"Oh, my God! Oh, thank God!" said the voice at the other end, excitedly. There was a few seconds' silence, during which the only sound she could hear was her father breathing into the receiver at the other end of the line. When he spoke again, he was in control of himself. "Thank God for that! Where are you calling from?"

"I can't tell you."

"What do you mean? Is that . . . that man still with you?"

"No, I'm on my own. I'll tell you about it later."

"Are you all right?"

"Yes. Yes, I'm quite all right. I just called so you wouldn't worry."

"But you're going home now, I trust! Judith, I hope you're going home now?"

"Yes, I'm going home now."

"Oh, my God! My dear girl, I'm so glad it's turned out like this! Judith, are you really sure you're all right?"

"Don't worry, Daddy."

"When will you be back?"

"As soon as I can manage it."

"Why do you sound so . . . so odd, Judith? Are you *sure* there's nothing wrong?"

"I'm terribly tired."

There was silence on the line for a moment and then the voice from Zürich spoke again. "Judith, are you there? Can you hear me?"

"Yes, Daddy."

"There's something I think I ought to tell you." Another pause, lasting several seconds, during which nothing could be heard but the sound of breathing. "There was an article in one of the papers, making disgraceful allegations, because it all went off so . . . so smoothly. They actually suggested it could have been a put-up job between you."

"It wasn't a put-up job, Daddy."

"You've not done anything wrong, have you?"

"I haven't done anything wrong, Daddy."

"I don't think I could have stood that, Judith. It would have been the end of everything. As manager of a firm like this, I can't afford the faintest breath of scandal—you do understand that, don't you, Judith?"

She did not reply; in fact, her vocal cords were so constricted that she was unable to utter a word.

"Judith, we haven't always seen eye to eye recently, but I think I'm right in saying that'll all be cleared up now. Am I right?"

"Yes, Daddy, you're right. It'll all be cleared up now."

"Have you spoken to your mother yet? You ought to call her. This business has made her ill."

"Tell her I haven't done anything wrong."

"Don't you want to tell her yourself? This would be the ideal moment to put things right with her, you know."

"I can't. Not now. I can't."

"Why not? For heaven's sake, you're seventeen years old! Be your age, can you?"

"I mean I literally can't, not at the moment. I'm in a hurry to catch a train."

"Oh, I see. I thought you meant you didn't want to. Well, of course—I'll call her myself, straight away.

This has made her really ill. She had to stay in bed this morning. Myself, I can't afford to stay away from work . . ."

She listened to the voice in the receiver, staring blindly at the wall of the telephone booth, where someone had scribbled a number. She heard the voice, but not the words. She hung up and left the telephone booth. She did not even notice the pain in her sore toe anymore. She walked slowly on to the platform and sat down on a shiny, red-painted seat. Something had happened to the world. Something had changed.

She took a cigarette out of the packet and lit it, but the smoke had no flavor; it smelled like the telephone booth. She threw the cigarette away, stood up, and walked slowly toward the exit of the station building.

The cloudy sky, lowering over the rooftops, cast a dull, gray light over the town. She threw the packet of cigarettes into a litter bin. Small coins jingled in her coat pocket as she walked mechanically along the pavement, her mind quite blank. She did not care which way she went. She stopped at a street corner where there was a supermarket, and stood there for some time, staring abstractedly at the cracks in the concrete of the pavement. Other passers-by had to avoid her. Finally she emerged from her trance, looked around, and went into the store. She had about twenty francs change left from her ticket. With the wire basket in her hand she walked past the self-service shelves, lost in thought. She bought a comb, a can of hair spray, and an American can of pineapple from Hawaii.

As she left the store, it was beginning to rain again, a fine drizzle.

14

The rain flowed over the stone roof, formed big drops and splashed down on the wet mud outside the door. He lay in the sleeping bag till nearly midday. Never before in his life had he felt so lonely and abandoned. A desert island? Yes, but one with warm white sand and green palm trees. Alone? Yes, but without any worries as to who had left that tin can standing in the stone trough. No fear of seeing a policeman suddenly appear in the doorway. He had never known time pass more slowly. Could it actually be standing still? He became restless, and felt he had to move. He crawled out of the sleeping bag, put on his shoes, hobbled outside with the help of his crutch, though his foot was hurting, and dipped his handkerchief in the icy water flowing out of the rusty pipe.

In the wet mist, the world had shrunk to a single stone building with two unglazed windows, a door falling off its hinges, a pile of hay and a few rotten planks of wood. He sat down on one of the planks and tied up his swollen ankle with the wet handkerchief. Then he hitched the rucksack toward him with the end of the crutch, put his hand down between the cans, and pulled out a bundle of banknotes. They were hundred-franc notes. Clumsily, he began to count them. When he got to thirty-two, he thought he might have made a mistake somewhere, but he went on counting; it struck him that the exact amount didn't really matter. He made it ninety-seven. Suppose he'd been three out—call it ten thousand, then. He went on to count the fifty-franc notes: they came to five thousand. Then he took out two more bundles of hundred-franc notes. When he got to forty-five thousand francs he had to stop and wipe his forehead with his elbow, because it was dripping with sweat. He made it forty-eight thousand in all. He did not even bother to count the twenty-franc notes, but just made a rough guess at them. Then he stuffed the notes back in the rucksack, leaned against the wall, and stared at a puddle in the mud outside the door. The only sounds to be heard were the splashing of raindrops and the rushing of the water as it ran down into the stone trough. The flush had faded from his cheeks. He tried to think how marvelous it was to have so much money, but his present surroundings were nothing marvelous . . . the place stank of old hay, mildew and dust, and outside there was only mist and rain.

He tried to think of plans for the future, but somehow he could not envisage peace and freedom, only a prison cell. He decided that cold and hunger were to blame for his dismal state of mind.

He got a can of goulash out of his rucksack, opened it, and picked out pieces of meat and jelly with the picnic fork. He loved canned goulash, and he told himself that now he could buy a hundred cans of goulash all at once. Or a hundred cans of Hawaiian pineapple. But today he was not really enjoying the goulash. He expected that that was because goulash ought to be eaten hot. Or was it because of the pain in his ankle? Or because, as he speared chunks of meat on his fork, he was keeping his ears pricked for any noises outside? He ate barely half of it, and left the rest, folding back the lid, which he had not quite removed. He licked the fork clean and put it back beside the tin. He'd warm the rest up in the evening. Goulash is really best hot.

Forty-eight thousand francs! Somewhere in the world, an earthly paradise must still exist. The problem was, how to get there? Well, he should be able to manage that, with forty-eight thousand in his pocket.

Taking his shoes off, he crawled back into the sleeping bag. Plenty of time yet to find his way to Paradise. He wished he could be like a bear, able to gorge himself and then hibernate all winter in some cave. He tried to persuade himself that everything was fine, and he was very happy. Forty-eight thousand! A ticket to Paradise! That was something to be pleased about, wasn't it? But somehow, Judith, somehow I feel miserable all the same . . .

He listened to the rain falling, the drops splashing into puddles, the water trickling out of the pipe. He listened until he fell asleep.

He woke toward evening, and stared stupidly at the door. He had had a wonderful dream. He had dreamed of sailing on board a ship to a new world, with Judith. It had been such a vivid dream that he still seemed to see her before his eyes. She was standing in the doorway, wearing the long raincoat, which was wet through, and her lovely golden hair hung lank at both sides of her face. She was holding her scarf. He sat up suddenly and stared at this wet vision, baffled. "Judith! Oh, God! It can't be possible!"

In the twilight, he could not see the expression on her face properly. "What happened?"

"Nothing," she said wearily. "I've brought you a can of pineapple. Here you are."

He stood up, leaning on his crutch. His legs were trembling as he went up to her. Was this really Judith? Judith had gone away for ever.

"Christ, I did want you to look back! I wanted you to turn around. Why have you come back?" He still expected to wake up any moment. "What happened?"

"Nothing happened," she said.

He saw that she was swaying on her feet, near collapse. He caught her by the elbows. The palms of his hands grasped the dampness of the coat, and when he bent his head slightly he could feel her wet hair on his face. He did not know what to say. He kissed the top of her head.

"I wish I were dead," she said. Her voice was desolate.

He helped her take off the wet coat, peeled off his thick pullover and put it over her head. She did not protest. She was apathetic. She sat on the worm-eaten plank he had laid across two logs of wood, and stared at the hard mud floor. A large, wet patch was collecting in the pale dust underneath the wet coat, now hanging from a rusty hook. He removed her sodden shoes and stuffed dry hay inside them, took two pairs of socks from the rucksack and got them on her feet. He warmed up the remains of the goulash on the spirit stove.

She ate obediently, though without enjoyment. They did not say a word the whole time. By now it was completely dark outside.

94

This was the moment, he thought, when he would find out what had actually happened. He was used to hard knocks; he knew that when anything pleasant seemed to happen you had to look for the drawbacks. He wondered if Judith had come back to have another go at persuading him to give himself up to the police. Or had she actually led the cops to him? A wave of heat ran through him at the mere idea. No, she wouldn't! She'd never do that! He hated himself; he felt as though he had laid filthy hands on something. He was used to dirt and double-dealing, but this was different. Something in the world had changed. He tried to think of the forty-eight thousand francs, unsuccessfully. Once again she was too close. Why had she come back?

"Judith, why did you come back? For Christ's sake, tell me!" He waited breathlessly for her answer. He felt that a great deal depended on that answer—maybe everything. He sat there beside her in the dark. He had to know for certain that she was there with him, and he also had to know the truth. He lifted his hand and touched hers. It was limp, lying there on the plank that formed their makeshift seat, and its palm was hot. He wondered if she were ill. She could have caught a chill; in this wet, cold, cheerless place she might get pneumonia, she might die, and it was all his fault for dragging her away from warmth and comfort and security to the cold, dirty world of criminals like himself. The mere idea horrified him.

"I can't go home," she said. She seemed to be fighting back tears. "I can't go home, ever."

"Why not?" He was feeling rather odd: weak and low-spirited.

95

"Don't ask. Please don't ask. I don't want to talk. I don't want to think. My head does hurt so much. I just want to sleep and sleep."

Bloody fool! he told himself. Idiot! Moron . . . !

"It'll all come right, Judith," he said, without conviction. Okay, he thought, so she has family problems —so what's it got to do with me? You'd better get out of this quick, chum—get as far away as you can, as fast as possible. Grab your forty-eight thousand and get out! He held her hot hand in his. He felt no excitement, no rush of blood to the head or anywhere else. He was not feeling sorry for her, he was feeling sorry for himself. He had suffered from bad attacks of self-pity ever since childhood. Never any luck; I always get the kicks. He let go of her hand and said, practically, "I've got some aspirin. Never without it! I don't trust any of the rest of that chemical muck, only aspirin. I'll make you some tea, and then you take a couple of aspirins and sleep it off, and tomorrow you'll be okay."

And that was the end of that. Or so he thought. But when he had made the tea, and she had obediently swallowed two aspirins and was lying in the sleeping bag, while he tried to keep warm by wearing two shirts and his jacket, burrowing into the old hay and covering himself with the damp coat, it started up again. He heard Judith ask him something quietly. He failed to catch it because of the hay rustling beneath his ear; he raised his head and listened. Her voice was trembling; her body was shaken by a shivering fit.

"Why did you want me to look around?" she repeated.

"Just some crazy idea I had."

"Did you want me to come back?"

"Yes," he said, and could have kicked himself for saying it.

"Why didn't you say so, then?"

"I'd have felt silly."

"I did want to look around," she said. Her teeth were chattering.

"Why didn't you, then?"

"I'd have felt silly too."

"Why *did* you come back?"

"I've got such an awful headache. I want to go to sleep."

After that, all he heard was her breathing. Her head was so close that when he reached out he could touch it. He felt her damp hair and burning forehead. There was hot, tender skin under his fingertips.

"Would you keep your hand there? My headache would be better then, and I could get to sleep," she said, in a weak, shaky voice.

He held the palm of his hand gently against her forehead, though his wrist began to ache unbearably after a while. But he stuck it out until he thought she really was asleep now.

Cautiously, he withdrew his hand and burrowed back into the hay. He thought of other girls he had known. It was not that he wanted to think of them; they forced their shameless way into his mind and refused to go away. A whole procession of them: he could do anything he liked with them, anywhere he wanted. On park benches in the evening. But with them, he had never felt anything like what he understood by the word "love," a word which he took to mean something extraordinary and wonderful, straight out of another world. So in the end he had come to think that "love" was really just another piece of gobbledygook for *that*. For something that was like eating. He remembered blonde Käthe. But Judith was different. And, to his own surprise, he realized that he too was different. He did not know what had happened to him, or exactly what had changed.

15

Overnight, the weather changed. The sky cleared, and in the morning the sun was shining. Everything did seem different in the sunlight. First and foremost, it was warm, and even the interior of the barn seemed less gloomy.

He made coffee on the spirit stove. He would not let Judith get up, but made her drink her coffee sitting up in the sleeping bag, and after breakfast he gave her more aspirin.

The sun had roused him from his uncertainties; he felt energetic and determined. The swelling on his ankle had gone down a lot, and the pain was almost gone. If he was careful not to put much weight on his right foot, he could get about without his crutch. Sun and warmth—yes, sun and warmth were the essentials of Paradise!

Judith was feeling better too. She sounded calmer this morning, though still depressed.

"I spoke to my father yesterday," she said suddenly.

He froze. He was holding a board, which he intended to make into a shelf so that he would not have to leave everything lying on the floor. "Where?" he asked, as calmly as he could. "Where did you speak to him?"

"At the station. On the phone."

"Oh, I see!" He was relieved, but he had to sit down for a moment. "What did you tell him? Did you say where you were calling from?"

"No, I didn't say."

"They can find out, though," he said, though he was not absolutely certain that this was so. "And then what?"

"I said I was going home."

"What did he say? Was he worried?"

"Yes, he was worried all right. Worried to death. Worried about the firm and his career. He's manager, and they're going to make him a director. No one's been talking of anything else at home lately."

He said nothing.

"His directorship, that's what he was really worried about. That's why I didn't go home. And I'm not going home again, ever. You do see, don't you?"

"Yes, Judith, I see," he said, though he didn't really. Such subjects had never come up at the Home or the approved school.

She went on, as if she were pouring out things that had been on her mind for years. "He only ever wanted to please her."

"Please who?"

"Her. That woman. I don't like her, and she doesn't like me either. She never did, right from the start."

He remembered all he had ever read about mother love. Not that he knew much about it himself; his own mother had died when he was four. However, this made him ask, "You don't like your mother?"

"She's not my mother. My real mother died when I was nine. That's too old to make such a big adaptation, don't you think?"

He didn't understand what she meant about an adaptation, but he said he agreed. Yes, she's got problems, he thought. Even rich people have problems! But family problems like this seemed strange and incomprehensible to him, and they did not really interest him. He had something very different on his mind. "Okay. So you don't want to go home. But why did you come back here?"

"That's just it. I don't exactly know," she said unhappily. "I haven't got anyone."

He remembered kissing her hair yesterday evening, and how he had wondered if she felt it, if she knew it had happened at all.

"I felt as though you were quite different from the others—I mean, different from everyone else," she went on. "I think being able to trust people is the most important thing of all. Do you know what I mean?"

"Yes, of course," he said firmly, feeling a fraud, because he was lying again. He didn't trust anyone much, even now. He was always inclined to be suspicious; like a dog, when he sensed something strange, something he didn't understand, his hair would stand on end and he would slink away.

"And my father said someone had written a piece in the paper saying it was probably a put-up job and I was in it with you."

After a moment's silence he said, indignantly, "What tripe! The bastards!"

They were both silent for a moment, and then he said grimly, "Well, you're in it now, Judith, right up to your neck. And I'm a bastard too, because I've been telling you to go home for three days, and I don't want you to go at all!"

"In case I tell the police where you're hiding?"

"No, Judith."

He limped outside the door.

Out in the sunshine on the south-facing slope it was warm and summery. The air was hazy with mist rising from the ground; it rose from the stone roof too, like smoke, as if there were a fire burning below the beams. The grass was still wet, but when they put a couple of planks on the ground they could lie side by side in the sun and get warm. Behind the barn there was a thick tangle of bushes, which gave way to grassy slopes, and far beyond and high above these slopes rose the rocky crags of the Alps. The narrow, stony path wound downhill to disappear somewhere in the valley far below. Up here it was safe and peaceful, and time passed gently by.

"I'm not surprised rich morons from all over the world come and build their villas in the south of Switzerland!" he said, though he was not really thinking of that.

Her mind was elsewhere, too. "You know, this isn't fair!" she said. "It's not right—you know all about me, and I don't know a thing about you!"

"That may be just as well!" he said, with mysterious significance. For one thing, he did not want to tell her about the approved school, and for another, he thought it would be more interesting to remain shrouded in mystery. But then it struck him that this was a bad way to treat another human being—the one human being in the world whom he really wanted to treat well.

"I'm just an ordinary crook, Judith, that's why I'm not all that keen to go on about myself," he said gloomily, but honestly. "I've stolen forty-eight thousand francs, with a pistol in my hand, like a gangster, and I've taken a hostage. But I don't have to tell you that. You know."

"You told me you weren't a thief. What did you mean?"

"You wouldn't understand."

"You keep saying that." She sounded bitter. "What makes you think I'm so feeble-minded?"

"Oh, Christ, Judith, I don't think that at all!" he said unhappily. "It's just that you don't know what the world's really like. Full of shit. You *can't* steal anything because it's all stolen already. There isn't any justice in the world. What do *they* call justice? Their own laws, right? I didn't make their laws. I don't recognize them! I want to be left alone, that's all." He did not want to mention his island paradise at the moment; he was too full of bitterness and distrust.

"Well, so what next?" she asked. "What are you going to do now?"

"Are *you* asking *me?*" he said in surprise. "I thought it'd be up to me to ask you!"

"I want to know what you think."

"Okay, I'll tell you. I think you want me to go to the police."

"That's right."

"And that's why you came back."

She was a long time answering, and he raised himself on one elbow to look at her face. She had closed her eyes, and small beads of sweat glistened on her fore-head and nose. Her blonde hair was shining again now that it was dry. A blonde, he thought, a goddam blonde! Suddenly he wanted to speak roughly to her, be coarse. Instead, he said quite quietly, "Judith, don't ever mention the police again."

He got up and limped into the barn to open a can. The can was hot already; it had been standing outside against the sunny wall all morning. He had thought of this as a way of economizing on fuel for the spirit stove. He did not want to light a fire in case anyone saw the smoke.

16

They did not mention the police again all that sunny afternoon, and neither of them mentioned the money either. They were both lost in their own thoughts, and they did not talk much. He could not help suspecting that Judith had still not told him everything. As the sun was going down behind the crest of the violet mountains he suddenly burst out violently, "Judith, I can't stand any more of this!"

"Any more of what?" The tone of his voice startled her, reminding her of the long-haired, bearded bandit.

"The uncertainty—I can't stand it! You haven't told me everything! You haven't told me how you went to the police!"

"You must be joking!" she said in a strangled voice.

He stopped short, and turned his face away, feeling ashamed of his outburst. "Yes, of course I'm joking!" he muttered. "Just thinking it could be true and you hadn't told me—that turns me right over! I don't know what's the matter with me," he added morosely. "Should be bloody *glad* to have got my hands on all that cash, *and* the only witness who could describe me to the police—hell, could even lead them right here!—and what do I do? I just keep thinking about you, Judith. Look, for Christ's sake, what's it got to do with me whether you can get on with some damn woman? So you're bored at home—so what? If I'd ever had a cozy little place like that, I'd have been a good little boy and kept my nose clean, you bet! You're one hell of a complication in my life, Judith. We never ought to have met."

He felt an almost physical pain as he spoke, and yet he couldn't help it, he had to go on, he had to be even tougher and more brutal with her. Looking deep into her eyes, he saw that he had hit her hard. That tender, Madonna-like face framed in the golden hair! "I've got enough problems of my own, Judith, and that's a fact. I couldn't care less if your father gets to be a director or not. It's all the same to me. Everything's all the same to me. I don't like people. I don't like anyone, see?"

He saw her face gradually change. Well, that was what he wanted; he was glad. He wanted to see her Madonna face distorted by weeping. He felt his heart beating violently, and something swelled up in his throat so that he had difficulty swallowing. "Matter of fact, I just don't fancy blondes, Judith."

Still it was not enough. He had to go on, go further, hurt her more. "I don't fancy girls at all, get it? So if you came back here so you could tell all your girl friends how you slept with a man on the run, that's your bad luck. You'll just have to tell them your bandit was a queer, won't you?"

His throat was dry as dust, his heart thudding violently, and he felt a painful pressure somewhere in the middle of his chest.

She said nothing at all. The soft features of her face

suddenly looked as if they were made of stone. Then she turned and ran, across the slope and along the path leading down to the valley.

"Judith!" he shouted, chasing after her. He disregarded the pain in his hurt leg; he ran as if his life depended on it, gasping and groaning, but still he ran with all his might. He caught up with her, and still running caught her by the elbow. She tried to tear herself free, but his fingers held her fast, like a hawk clutching its prey. Gasping for air, he tried to say something, but all he could get out was her name.

She was exhausted too, but as soon as she had recovered slightly she tore herself violently away and began to run again. He followed, and caught up with her once more. This time he put both arms around her. She struggled desperately, slipped on the wet grass and fell backwards. He threw himself on her, grasped both her wrists, and held her down. She lay there on her back, arms stretched wide, as if crucified. Fighting for breath, he managed to utter a few disjointed words.

"Judith . . . not true . . . you know it isn't true . . ."

With the last of her strength she tried to free herself. She struggled half upright several times, and then gave it up and lay there quite still, her eyes closed. He leaned over her face and began to kiss her eyes, her cheeks and her lips. She did not resist.

"Judith, you don't really believe it, do you? What I said? I only said it because I love you so much. I never thought there could be anything like this. But I do now. I loved you right from the very first moment, Judith. I just want to keep on and on saying it, how much I love you, and you must believe me—I'll just

107

keep on saying it, Judith, on and on saying it—Judith, oh, Judith!"

He let go of her wrists, collapsed on the grass and laid his head beside hers.

They lay side by side in the wet grass for quite a long time, silent and still. At last he said huskily, "Judith, you mustn't lie on the damp ground. It's getting chilly."

Leaning on his left arm, he touched her face gently with his right hand. He could feel something wet on his hand. He bent over her and gently wiped her tears away with his fingers. "Can you ever forgive me, Judith? For what I said just now?"

She did not reply, only raised her limp hand and ran her fingers through his thick hair.

"Do you love me?" he asked. "I have to know."

For the first time she opened her eyes. "Don't you know? Really?"

He helped her up, and they went slowly back to the barn. Its stone walls were rosy in the evening light. He had to lean on her arm; the exertion had made his leg hurt again.

"What bloody luck for us both. Meeting this way," he said. He felt as though Fate had set a cunning trap for him. Then he realized that Judith was trembling. He touched her forehead; it was hot.

"What now?" she asked. She had asked the same question earlier that day, but this time it sounded as if she meant it to apply to both of them.

They sat side by side on the makeshift bench, holding hands.

"What are we going to do?" she asked, for the third time.

"We've got a choice. Either we give up and go to the police—and I go to jail—and then maybe begin all over again. Or we go through with it."

"How can we go through with it?" she asked, in a voice trembling with fever and emotion.

"We could go away together. Somewhere very far away."

"I'd like that. With you. Somewhere very far away —far away from here. But I don't have any papers, have you thought of that? No passport, nothing."

"But we've got money." He wondered where he could get hold of a forged passport. He didn't know anyone in these parts, but he could find someone in Germany. However, this was all very vague. He needed time to work it out. "And then we'll always be together, Judith. Just the two of us."

He thought hard. Where *could* he find out how to lay hands on a forged passport? Anything can be done, if you have the money.

"Were you thinking about an island?" she asked and her teeth chattered.

"Mm. Our island, Judith. Just for the two of us."

"Do you really think there are any islands like that left?" She sounded as if she hoped desperately that there were.

"Yes, there *are* still places like that, Judith. Only a long way away. You need money to get there, and we've got money." He thought of people who might be able to help him, and he remembered Gustl—stammering Gustl, from Münich. "Gustl!" he exclaimed.

"Who's Gustl?"

"Someone I know. In Münich. Gugu—he'll get hold of a forged passport for you. He'd do anything for money." He felt relieved, as if he had found a solution to everything.

"Does it *have* to be a forged passport?" she asked unhappily.

"Well, for Christ's sake, Judith, of course it does!"

"It just sounds so horrible—forged passport!"

"Don't let that bother you. Be like me. The world's a rotten place—hasn't that ever struck you? Jesus Christ, has that *really* never struck you?"

"I suppose you're right. I just wish I could be somewhere very far away now, this minute."

"You can't, not now. Now I must make you some hot lemon tea, and then you have an aspirin. You've got to get better, that's the main thing now."

"Yes. Yes, I like lemon tea."

She was overtaken by such a fit of shivering that she could not even get hold of the zipper when she wanted to take off her skirt and crawl into the sleeping bag. He had to help her.

"Don't look," she said, as he helped her out of her skirt.

"Don't worry, Judith. I'll be good to you."

"You are good to me."

He helped her zip up the sleeping bag and smoothed her hair back on both sides of her face. Then he made tea. Judith, docile now, took two aspirins and drank the tea. Her body was still shaken by the shivering until the hot drink and the drug began to take effect. She wanted him to put his hand on her forehead, like the night before. She was quieter now, but her breathing still came fast and shallow. He lay beside her, his palm against her forehead, waiting for her to drop off to sleep. After about a quarter of an hour, she asked, "Why did you say you were queer?"

He did not know what to say.

"I wanted you to hate me. I wanted to hurt you somehow."

"Why?"

"Because I love you so much."

"I love you too, but I don't want to hurt you."

He sat up and kissed her closed eyelids several times.

"So why? Why did you want to hurt me?" she asked again.

"We're different sort of people, Judith. I'm a man, for one thing."

"But you're not queer, are you?"

"No, I'm not, Judith," he said, stroking her forehead. The sweat of fever was beginning to break out on it, and he thought it would be a good idea for him to get up and soak a handkerchief in cold water.

"I'm going to give you a compress on your forehead. We want you to get better as soon as possible."

"All right," she said obediently.

He stood up and limped away to moisten the handkerchief. When he came back she asked, in a weak, drowsy voice, "Did you look when you were taking off my skirt?"

"Yes, I looked. Anyway, you're wearing tights," he said, putting the cold compress on her forehead.

"Why did you look, when I asked you not to?"

"Because I love you, Judith."

"Yes, I know. But I like to hear you say it."

"Well, I'm going to keep on saying it. Till you've heard enough of it!"

At last her breathing came more slowly, and she fell asleep. He did not feel sleepy. The events of the last few hours kept going around and around in his head, like a set of film clips being shown over and over again. So this is what it's really like, he told himself. Judith, Judith . . . He could think of nothing but her name.

Later, when Judith woke, he gave her another aspirin. She was thirsty, so he limped out to the pipe and the constant trickle of water from it. As water flowed into the tin can he gazed at the moonlit mountains. The place looked like a film set. But the can brought his mind firmly back to reality. He wondered what he would do if someone turned up at the barn the next day.

"I had a horrible dream," said Judith, when she had drunk the water. "I dreamed we were on a big ship together, with crowds of people, and I lost you. But people can't possibly get lost on a ship, can they?"

"No, of course not. That's why I'm here, Judith!"

He tossed and turned uneasily in the rustling hay, thinking about a forged passport for Judith. He did not drop off to sleep until nearly morning, and then he dreamed of the police. The fuzz. The bastards.

17

Next day was a day of contrasts. It was sunny and warm—and Judith was ill. He hoped it was just a touch of summer flu brought on by the changeable weather. He still had six aspirins left in the box; he hoped the little white tablets were powerful enough to combat this wretched germ. He could hardly believe his luck, having Judith here with him, but he knew that she was going to present quite a complication over the next few days. He was worried, but he tried to hide it from her. He did not want her getting up; people with flu are supposed to stay in bed to shake it off. But maybe it isn't flu at all, he thought, maybe it's just a cold.

"You oughtn't to sit in the sun when you have a temperature," he told her.

"How do you know I've got a temperature?"

They argued for a while as to whether or not Judith had a temperature. Finally she admitted that perhaps she did have a slight temperature, and she would stay where she was, so as to get better more quickly. "But you must stay here with me, and tell me about yourself."

"That'd be as bad as the flu!" he said, trying to make a joke of it. "I don't want to make you worse!"

"All right. Tell me about your islands, then."

He thought of the cans of food. How long would they last two people? He had not reckoned on double rations. But in three or four days' time his foot might be better, and he could go down and buy some food. And he was sure Gugu could get hold of a passport. Gustl would do anything in the world for money.

"Are you listening, Peter?"

"Yes, I'm listening, Judith—the thing is, I'm lazy in the mornings, see? I don't feel like talking." The islands seemed a long way off now, but Judith was close. He lay down on the hay beside her. Sunlight flooded in through the window, with motes of bright dust floating in it like stars in a miniature universe.

"Do you feel very bad?" he asked anxiously.

"No, I'm fine when you're here with me."

He bent down and began to kiss her, with passion this time, feeling her soft hands on his cheeks. And suddenly he remembered Hermine—fat Minna, daft Minna, the caretaker's daughter. Minna knew a thing or two, though. He was eleven years old, and in the Home where they were supposed to be improving his character. It was Sunday morning, a hot summer day out of doors, and it was hot in the attic too. He had crept up there in secret. The old packing cases behind which he was hiding had a funny smell, a smell of resin and dust and something else—he could not put a name to it, but he never forgot it afterwards. He had brought out an envelope full of well-thumbed photographs with dogeared, crumpled corners from its hiding place under his shirt. They were pornographic pictures. Someone had smuggled them into the Home, and now a circle of conspirators were passing them around from hand to hand. The bright, summery light fell into the attic through a skylight in the roof. Then he heard a sound. He froze in alarm, thinking one of the grown-ups must have spotted him, and pressed close to a packing case, peering cautiously through a crack. He saw Minna in the dim light near the door. She was barefoot, carrying her shoes; he supposed she didn't want anyone to hear her. He held his breath, wondering what would happen next, in the grip of a strange excitement, for the attic seemed full of a mysterious, forbidden, shameful Something emanating from those photographs. There was no chance of escaping unseen, so he didn't even try it. Through his crack, he watched Minna quietly approach the packing cases. She must have been spying on him. She knew he was there. Sure enough, she was suddenly right there beside him. Four years older than he was, a head taller, and almost twice as heavy. Fat, daft Minna, with a grin of triumph on her flushed, sweaty face. Perhaps she wasn't so daft after all. Perhaps that was just what people said.

"What are you doing here?" she said. "You know no one's allowed up here."

"Nothing to do with you!" he answered back. "Mind your own business!" His fingers were clutching the envelope of photographs behind his back.

"What've you got there? What's that you're hiding?" she asked suspiciously, grabbing the hand he was holding behind his back.

He tried to push her off, but she was too heavy. She hugged him like a bear so as to get her hands around behind his back, and her big, prematurely developed breasts pressed against his face. He was revolted and bewildered. He fought desperately for possession of the envelope of photographs.

"Fat old bag!" he gasped, as he felt his strength ebbing.

She let go of him, swung back her hand and slapped his face. He stumbled over a corner of the packing case and fell. The pictures flew all over the tiled floor.

She snatched them quickly, before he could get up. Her face was triumphant. "Just what I thought! Everyone likes this sort of thing!"

"Give them back!" he said, holding out his hand.

Oddly, he felt neither fear nor anger. There was something mysterious and obscene in the atmosphere of the attic, linking them together.

"And suppose I don't?" she said. She was standing in front of him, and he could feel his ears and face going red. He had a sudden impulse to take hold of the two mounds of flesh swelling under the bodice of her dress.

"Suppose I don't give them back?" she repeated. It was a meaningless question, and they both knew it.

He took a determined step forward. He was very close to her now; he noticed that she was swallowing hard.

"Hand them over, or you'll see!" he managed to say.

"I'm not afraid of you. You're afraid of me, though!"

"What for? Why should I be afraid of you?" In the hot air of the attic, he felt as though a strange glow were coming from her. She moved, and he felt her hand, felt her put it down the waistband of his trousers, felt it travel downwards, feeling him there, under his stomach. A wave of unbearable heat swept over him.

He didn't know quite what had happened, or how much time had passed. When he found himself sitting on the floor, staring at her splayed legs and distorted face, listening to her noisy, gasping breath as her moans gradually subsided, he felt revulsion and a deep disappointment. The wood of the packing cases smelled strange, and the world seemed appallingly empty . . .

Judith was running her long, slim fingers through his hair. Why did he have to go and remember that, just now? He had never liked remembering it, and today the memory seemed nothing short of blasphemy. He had cooled off. He laid his head beside Judith's, and then at once moved a little further away. He was afraid of being so close to her. He felt as though the thoughts in his head might somehow be communicated to hers— a horrifying idea. He took a lock of her hair in his hand and let it run through his fingers. It was pretty hair. Much prettier than Käthe's. It was naturally blonde, not the result of mucking about with chemicals. Käthe had once come late to their meeting place, bathed in sweat from hurrying, because he liked her to be on time. Her red face made an odd contrast with her dyed hair, and for the first time he got the impression that her hair was a kind of mask; there was something false about it. However, he was sixteen at the time, and quite crazy about Käthe. All that winter they used to go to a bar with a jukebox. They held hands when they walked through the streets, but he never kissed her in the street. He felt awkward about kissing her in public. In the park, yes—in the park they hugged and kissed, though that was all, because he still could not get rid of his mental image of Minna lying there moaning and gasping. He thought real love should be something quite different. Then he discovered that Käthe was going out with Freddy at the same time, but on different days. Going out with that trendy-looking, perverted bastard! Freddy had told everyone what he, Freddy, did with Käthe on a bench in the park, adding that all blondes were hot stuff, really hot. His parting from Käthe had not gone off very well. Instead of slapping her face, as he had meant to do, he found himself left standing while she marched off like an insulted princess, saying by way of a parting shot that she'd had enough of his twaddle about Tahiti anyway —he was already talking about Tahiti—*and* his dirty hands which stank of the garage. He scrubbed his nails carefully to get the black grease out, wore plastic gloves and rubbed hand-cream in after work. And after that, he used to take willing girls to the park, and did the things with them that Freddy and Käthe did on park benches. That was his revenge. One day he met Käthe in the street, with some other bastard, someone he didn't know. She had her arm around his waist, and she looked so ordinary that he wondered why he'd ever thought so much of her. What had been the matter with his eyes? Her pretty face and her fair hair were all the result of some chemical muck . . .

"What are you thinking?" ask Judith.

"I was thinking that the cans will run out in a few days. I'll have to go and buy some food. I just hope my foot'll be okay."

"I've been nothing but a nuisance to you, right from the start," she said unhappily.

He began to kiss her again. He desperately wanted to forget all his worries, and he thought she felt the same. He could feel their mutual longing passing from their lips into his head, all along his backbone, over his whole body and back again, with growing intensity.

"Are you sure you're feeling all right, Judith?" he asked, in a voice that he could barely control.

"I feel fine, with you here . . ."

He unzipped the sleeping bag with a jerky movement and lay down beside her. "I want to get closer to you."

She said nothing. She still said nothing while he struggled desperately with the memory of Minna gasping on the floor. He must not close his eyes. He had to see that this was Judith. And he did it: he managed to forget the past.

Afterwards they lay side by side, their breath coming more slowly, as tiny motes of dust floated in the slanting column of sunlight. "Do you think it was just chance, us meeting?" he asked.

Somehow the world seemed lit by a different light now. Everything looked different. Everything *was* different.

"I don't know. I don't want to think about anything just now, only about you being here."

A little later, she said, "You know what would really have been awful? If you'd really been queer."

"Yes," he said, hugging her. "But I'm not."

"I know, but it would have been awful, all the same. You were horrible yesterday. Just for a little while you were really horrible."

"And I'm not horrible today?"

"No, not today," she said, putting her arms around him. "But I didn't really believe it, anyway, because I didn't want to believe it."

"Because you knew I loved you?"

"Because I hoped you loved me."

"Well, you know now." He felt the excitement of her body begin to communicate itself to him again, through the touch of his hands. This time, he was able to close his eyes and still know it was Judith. There was nothing left but the present.

Warm air streamed into the old barn from outside, air from the plains of Italy or all the way from the hot shores of Africa. They lay side by side, eyes closed, with hot white sand and gently rustling palm trees around them. They were on an island, just the two of them. But soon they returned to the mainland. "How many girls have you had?" Judith asked reflectively. "I mean, how many.*really* . . ."

He had been expecting some such question, but it took him by surprise all the same, because he had just been thinking along similar lines. How many men had she been with? He felt cornered, in spite of having anticipated the question. He didn't want to lie to her, but he did not want to tell the truth either.

"Why do you want to know?" he asked, playing for time.

"Because when people love each other they can tell each other anything. Everything. They *have* to tell each other everything."

"Okay. You tell me about yourself, and then I'll believe there aren't any secrets between us," he said cravenly.

She said no more for a while; no doubt she was feeling cornered too. Then, summoning up her courage, she said, "My first time was when I was fourteen. So you can see what I'm like! Still, that's when it was.

One holiday . . . do I have to tell you all the details?"

"No, Judith, you don't have to."

"I was silly, and curious. And dreadfully disappointed afterwards."

"I was disappointed too," he said, more boldly now. "Only I was just eleven!"

"No! It isn't possible!"

"I don't like thinking about it." Suddenly he felt enormously relieved, as if he had got rid of a heavy burden.

"What about the others?"

"You first!"

"Coward!—Oh, all right. I left the man I was sleeping with six months ago. He was the second. I haven't had anyone since. He wasn't interested in anything else. I hated him."

"Don't you hate me now?" he asked uneasily.

"Something's different. I don't know what, but it all seems different now. It must be because I love you so much." She ran her fingers through his thick hair, and he thought he had got off lightly, but he was wrong. "Now, go on then, Casanova! Eleven!"

With some difficulty, he mastered his jealousy of the man she had left six months before. Her own frankness put him to shame, but he dared not talk about his own past. "I knew this blonde, a few years back . . ." he began, hesitantly.

"Prettier than me?" she interrupted.

"Not pretty at all. She wasn't even a genuine blonde, she dyed it. In fact she was a sham right the way through." Better not go on about Käthe. No reason to, after all. He supposed he ought to tell her about the park benches, but he found he couldn't. He felt that he must not lie, but he was unable to tell her all the truth.

She sensed that something was troubling him. "Right, so she was a sham. Never mind her, then!" she said generously. "How about the others?"

A sense of regret came over him. He felt dirty, degraded. "It was all just dirty, till I found you. Why talk about it? I was just bloody disappointed—do you know what I mean?"

"Yes, I know. I won't disappoint you, ever."

"I won't disappoint you either, Judith. I'm not so bad really," he said, hoping that was the truth, or at least half the truth. Or not too black a lie.

She tugged at his hair, pulling his head down toward her, and kissed him on the nose. "I found *that* out before you did. If I didn't know that, would I be going off to somewhere the other side of the world with you?"

"You're the first one, really," he said softly. This time he was telling the truth, for the past was gone.

Judith did not want anything to eat that evening. Her face was flushed with fever, and she swallowed two aspirins and drank some tea.

"Put your hand on my forehead. Then I'll be all right."

He lay beside her with his hand on her hot forehead, listening anxiously to her breathing. Paradise had receded again. It was very far away.

18

Thursday. The sound of a dog, barking furiously, woke them next morning. It sounded so close the dog could have been barking right inside the barn. Peter flung back the coat, under which he had been lying, and began to struggle to get his trousers on. His ankle was hardly swollen at all now, but he could not bend his leg properly yet, and he had difficulty getting his tight jeans on in a hurry. It occurred to him that it didn't really matter if they arrested him with or without his trousers on. He was sorry the dream was coming to an end so soon. Most of all, he was sorry about Judith.

Exhausted by her feverish night, Judith lay still in the sleeping bag, watching him with mingled fear and grief as he struggled with his trousers. In the bright morning sun he could see the blue circles around her eyes. She looked really ill. This alarmed him even more than the thought of the police. He managed to produce a faint smile for her. It was a goodbye smile, or meant to be.

However, when at last he had his trousers on and limped over to the door, he saw a big, mottled dog on the doorstep, the kind that Alpine shepherds use for herding sheep and cows. The dog bared its teeth and barked in a deep voice. Peter picked up his crutch and tried to shoo it away. The animal retreated, but went on barking.

When he got outside the door, he saw a man coming down the grassy slope above the barn. The man called to the dog. He was obviously a shepherd. He had a bag hanging over his shoulder, and a military type of metal canteen in his hand. As he came closer he called out a greeting in Italian.

Peter replied in German, and there was an awkward silence, during which he tried to adjust to this new situation. Only now did he begin to shake inwardly with emotion. They might make it yet!

The man, who was around forty, was short but broad-shouldered, his round head set on a short, strong throat and neck. Pointing to his canteen, he said something in Italian.

"Water," said Peter reluctantly, pointing to the stone trough. He disliked men of this type, full of animal magnetism.

"I know," said the shepherd, in German. He called something out in Italian, and the dog stopped barking.

"Good water, that," said the shepherd, smiling, as he went over to the rusty pipe. The dog growled menacingly. The shepherd took a small can of orange juice from his bag, opened it, and poured its contents into the canteen, which he filled up with water. "This is good when it's hot," he said, slapping the canteen. "The water up there's useless—must flow through a muddy patch somewhere." He spoke good German, with no Swiss accent. He was looking Peter up and down with interest. Then he caught sight of a pair of lady's black shoes on the window sill, and laughed knowingly, closing one eye.

The dog was drinking from a puddle at the foot of the stone trough.

"We were out hiking yesterday—my wife got something the matter with her foot, so we had to spend the night here," explained Peter.

"I see, I see!" said the shepherd, laughing again. "Good fun, hiking, eh?" He held up his fingers in an obscene gesture, winking in a knowing way once more.

In other circumstances Peter would have laughed, but not here and now. He felt disgust for the man, and turned away, looking grim.

The shepherd said something to his dog and prepared to move off. "Shoes like that are no good for the mountains!" he said. He added something in Italian, and went away.

Peter watched thoughtfully as the man slowly climbed up the slope back to his pastures.

"Who was that?" Judith asked when he came back inside the barn. She was standing in the middle of the floor, barefoot, but wearing her blouse and skirt. Plainly she had not wanted to be found lying in the hay.

"A shepherd, coming to get water. He's gone now." He tried to make light of it. Belatedly, he noticed that she was dressed, and he was struck again by the look of illness in her eyes. "Why did you get up? You must sleep all day today, then you'll be better tomorrow."

"I didn't want anyone to find me in the hay," she said apologetically. "They might have thought . . . might have thought anything!"

"That wouldn't have bothered me! *I* thought there were at least twenty armed cops outside when I heard that dog!"

She was still standing barefoot on the hard mud floor; the general effect of her long, slender legs, short black skirt and white blouse was an exotic one in this primitive, tumbledown place.

Very different feet must have trodden on this mud floor, he thought, looking at her, and he thought of the police armed with pistols, and wished there was warm, white sand under her slim feet, instead of a hard mud floor. He remembered the shepherd and his rude gesture, and hated the man. This was Judith, not Minna!

"I don't think he'll tell anyone about us," he said, as if to encourage himself.

"Us?" she queried. "He didn't see me."

"No, but he saw your shoes."

She was taken aback. "Do you suppose he thought we were—were doing anything?"

"Maybe he doesn't read the papers or listen to the radio," he said, still trying to encourage himself. He hoped to God that shepherd *didn't* read the papers or listen to the radio. He wished the man were a helpless idiot, illiterate, unable to read or write. He wished he were deaf and dumb! However, he knew that all this was just wishful thinking. He hoped the man was not too bright, anyway; he couldn't be very bright, surely, or he wouldn't be stuck in a job like this at his age, herding sheep up a lonely mountain? Or did that just show how wise he was?

"I didn't mean that. I don't like to think of him imagining us here in the hay together."

"Why would he think about that?" he said, remembering the shepherd's gesture with disgust.

"I'm sure he did."

"Oh, never mind what he thinks! The hell with him!" he said, suddenly impatient. "Just so long as he doesn't go shooting his mouth off to anyone."

"I've only made trouble for you, all along," she said miserably.

He hugged her and kissed her hot cheek. "Don't worry, Judith. Don't worry about anything. You must lie down and take an aspirin. It's no good you being ill, or . . ." He was about to say, jokingly, that if she was ill he wouldn't take her to his island, but suddenly he did not feel like joking. Anyway, it was not much of a joke; it contained too much irony for comfort.

"Or what?" she asked.

"If you were ill, we'd have to throw it all up. Everything."

"Not *everything*, maybe," she said quietly, trying to manage a smile. It was the same slightly sentimental smile he remembered from the face of the Madonna hanging up among the nudes. "Maybe not everything," she repeated. "Not having met each other, when the world's so full of people. I don't want anything to part us again, ever. What did you mean about having to throw it all up?"

He paused before replying, seeing a whole crowd of policemen, judges and warders in his mind's eye. A cell window looking out on a prison yard, and through the bars you could see white clouds, driven by the wind, sailing far away. "I want to take you somewhere very far away, Judith. That's all. That's why you have to get well."

"I've only got a bit of a cold. We can start now if you like."

He looked into her eyes for a long time, wishing that what she said was true. But he knew it was not. He knew, moreover, that there was more to getting somewhere very far away than just boarding a train or a ship or an aircraft. Even with a bundle of good Swiss francs in your pocket. He would dearly have liked to get away from this wretched barn as fast as possible. How the shepherd had gawked at the pair of shoes in the window! But a person with a temperature is not supposed to move around much, in case of pneumonia. Pneumonia without medical help—Christ, no! For a split second he thought how simple everything would be if he were on his own. It was only a momentary, half-formed idea, and he instantly thrust it away from him like something unclean.

"And if I'm too much of a nuisance you can go on your own," she said, making a great effort.

He was rooted to the spot. Christ, he thought, it isn't possible! She guesses it all! She knows everything! Perhaps the brain can broadcast and receive messages like a radio set!

"I don't even want to think of that, Judith," he said truthfully. "I don't want to be alone again. God, I've always been alone. How could you think I'd leave you? You didn't really mean it, did you?"

"No, I didn't really mean it," she said apologetically. She was so weak from the fever that she swayed as she took off her skirt.

"Please don't look."

"I'm going to look! I'm going to look at you all day and all night till we get to our island. You won't be able to stop me—you know what I'm like!"

He tried to make a joke of it, to cheer her up.

"Oh, if only we were somewhere a long, long way away," she sighed.

He covered her up carefully, lay down on the hay beside her, and put his hand on her forehead.

"Now I know you're there, even with my eyes

closed," she said. "I don't care what that shepherd thinks about us—what a million people think about us. You're my whole world now."

When she was asleep he lay quietly beside her, afraid to move for fear of waking her. From down there on the floor he could see deep blue sky through the window. It was a familiar color to him; he had often seen it arched above the sea from horizon to horizon.

19

He was on board a white ship, leaning on the white-painted rail. Judith was leaning on his shoulder, and her hair, blowing in the wind, whipped his face gently. The ship was large and luxurious, although he had originally intended to travel on a small vessel with few passengers. A freighter, for preference, putting in at every port. But Judith wanted a big white ship. Judith came from a completely different world. She was elegantly dressed, like the people in the Bahnhofstrasse in Zürich, and she was pleased because she attracted attention. He did not mind; in fact he was proud of her. He liked to show her off, knowing that she was really all his and no one else's.

His own clothes were casual. He wore faded blue jeans, partly because he liked to provoke people by being unconventional, partly because he thought a man of the world should have a mind above his trouser creases. His own mind was not only above trouser creases, but this whole, elegant world—apart from the elegant Judith.

It struck him that one of the ship's officers was looking at Judith a good deal too much. Judith was well aware of it, too, a fact which did not escape him either. He felt annoyed about it.

"That lout's hardly taken his eyes off you for a whole week," he said, coolly. "I've had about enough of this." He remembered seeing an old film in which Gary Cooper, when angry, clenched his teeth so that his cheek muscles stood out, thus showing that he was exercising great self-control. Peter clenched his teeth several times.

"Who? What lout?" she asked, pretending not to understand.

"You know very well what lout! The one with the gold stripe on his sleeve."

"Well, suppose he *is* looking at me? Where's the harm in that?"

"You like him, the moron, don't you? That's where the harm is!" he said with icy calm.

"You must be joking!"

"I must be joking, must I? *I* can see the way you look at him. I may well find myself knocking your fancy man's teeth in pretty soon, and that won't be any joke either!"

She went pale. He must have struck home. "I didn't know you could be so—so tough!" she said.

She turned her head away, and he knew she was beginning to cry. The people walking on deck turned their heads curiously, and whispered. He knew what they were whispering about. Judith and the ship's officer!

"Yes, I'm tough all right. On account of growing up in the Home, that's why. Your fancy man there's from a grand family. Dear old Daddy's a company director." (What exactly does a company director do, anyway?)

He clenched his jaw, and the muscles of his cheek rippled. "Well, now I'm going to give you a little lesson in good conduct!"

He was very cool, very casual. He gripped Judith's hand so tight that she moaned faintly with the pain, and he led her over to the officer. She went with him unwillingly, hanging back, for she was afraid something dreadful was going to happen, but his fingers held her hand in a steely grip. He had once seen Gary Cooper drag his unfaithful girl friend out of a bar, while she beat at his unmoving face with her little fists, as if she were hitting a stone statue—fantastic! But Judith was different, less temperamental. Submissive tears were more her line.

The officer seemed to have realized that something was up, for he looked around at the other passengers rather uncertainly as the two of them came up to him. No doubt he sensed that something dramatic was about to occur. He tried to see what it was from Judith's eyes, but Judith had bent her head and was staring at the planks of the deck. They stood there like conspirators caught in the act.

"I take it you're not on duty at the moment, sir?" said Peter, smiling politely. He was pleased to see the officer's face flush with suppressed anger.

"You are correct, sir," replied the officer, in arrogant tones, bowing slightly to Judith.

"Then perhaps you'd care to have a drink with us, sir?"

"With pleasure, sir," said the officer coolly, never taking his eyes off Judith.

She raised her head at last, and their glances met. Peter increased the pressure of his steely fingers. The officer laughed, embarrassed, and they all three went down to the ship's bar.

They sat on tall stools, Judith in the middle, drinking whisky and soda, sipping their drinks slowly. The bar was usually empty in the morning except for two or three alcoholics, taking in their daily ration at their leisure. Today, the place was full. Passengers came in singly, or in small groups, smiling enigmatically, their ears pricked, their eyes watchful.

"I asked you to come down here to spare you unpleasantness in front of inquisitive onlookers, sir," said Peter, playing with his glass on the bar counter. "I'd no idea it would be so full today," he added apologetically.

"I don't know what you're talking about," said the officer, looking nervously around the bar.

"Oh, but I think you do, sir," said Peter, with an amiable smile. Judith put her hand on his, but he flung it off impatiently. "I want you to apologize to my wife. She says you've been bothering her."

"You must be drunk!" said the officer offensively, pushing away his half-empty glass and getting up to leave.

"Just a moment," said Peter calmly. "That's not all. When I was coming out of this bar yesterday evening I saw you in the passage outside my wife's cabin. She had a headache; she needed to rest. Are you telling me you were on duty outside that cabin so that my wife could rest?"

"What are you getting at? What's all this supposed to mean?"

"*I'm* asking *you* what all this is supposed to mean," he said icily.

"For God's sake, madam, say something!" The officer turned to Judith.

"Are you suggesting that my wife *invited* you in?" asked Peter, with a vicious glance. He felt they were both in his power now. His cheek muscles quivered from time to time with a kind of dreadful joy.

The ship's officer was so confused that he did not know what to say or do. Trying to save the situation, he laughed out loud. "I almost fell for it! Rather an unusual sort of joke, sir! I admit, I almost fell for it. I began by taking you seriously. However, I hope that will be all. I must be going." He looked at the gold watch on his wrist.

"No, don't do that!" said Peter. He laughed too. "You see, the real reason I invited you down here was to smash your face in."

"Peter!" cried Judith, seizing his hand. He pushed her hand away, keeping his eyes on his enemy's face. He saw the man's teeth, bared in a painfully forced smile, which contrasted strangely with the hatred in the pale blue eyes half hidden by narrowed lids. He wondered, if those two ever had children, what color their eyes would be. "Take a good look at your handsome lover here!" he told Judith harshly. "See how brave he is! Standing there laughing like a jackass instead of trying to knock my teeth in!"

At this the officer stopped laughing, leaned across Judith, and swung his fist violently. Peter did not flinch away, but sat there still as a statue while the fist made contact with his left cheek. Everyone in the bar was transfixed. It was perfectly quiet, just like a scene in a film. Peter and the officer got off their tall bar stools, and the officer began to retreat slowly toward the exit from the bar, with Peter following slowly. The bunched muscles rippled above his jawline. Judith tried to bar his way, but he pushed her away with a single movement, so violently that she fell to the ground. The officer kept retreating, bewildered, until he found himself up against a wooden wall. He spread both hands, as if to support himself against the wall, and stared wide-eyed at the big man approaching him, his arms hanging by his sides, a cold, indifferent expression on his face. The officer closed his eyes. The sound of two sharp blows rang out in the deathly silence.

Judith, who had got up from the shiny parquet floor of the bar by now, ran to Peter's side and tugged at his hand, which was grasping the lapel of the officer's uniform jacket. Peter's right hand rose, and the palm made contact with the officer's face again. And at last he knew who that arrogant face reminded him of. The man was the image of the Head of the Home! The officer did not defend himself. Paralysed by fear, he leaned back against the wall, his head swaying from left to right in time to the regular blows. Judith tried to stop that merciless right hand, but it was like a child trying to stop some unfeeling machine. She began hammering at Peter's shoulder with her fists, and then, tears of desperation in her eyes, at his head too. But he looked like a stone statue. He felt nothing, nothing touched him, he was incredibly calm. He just went on hitting his rival's face slowly, at measured intervals, looking exactly like Gary Cooper the whole time . . .

"Peter," Judith groaned softly, "could you get a wet handkerchief and wipe my face? I'm sweating all over. It must be the aspirin."

He got up from the hay and went to moisten the handkerchief in the stone trough. Then he wiped her soft face and forehead, and kissed both her eyes.

135

"Could it be infectious?" she asked anxiously. "It would be dreadful if you caught it and got ill."

"Don't worry, Judith." He stroked her golden hair. He wished desperately that he had some miraculous healing power in his hand. Some people do have such a gift. "The worst's over now," he said—firmly, because he wanted to believe it himself. He let his fingers roam among the locks of her hair. His fingertips touched her delicate skin, and he tried to believe that all this was not just a hallucination, or a vision or a dream. Judith, Judith, Judith. He felt as though her name were imprinted on every cell in his body.

"I do love you so much," she said softly. "I almost feel as if I'd like to die."

"Don't say such things!" he cried, horrified.

" I don't mean literally. It's just a sort of feeling. I can't explain it any other way. I'd like to hold on to it always. And never lose you."

"You won't ever lose me, because I won't ever lose you. You do believe me, don't you?"

"Yes, I do. And you won't lose me either. Do you believe that?"

He thought of the ship's officer; he bent over her face and kissed her. "Yes, Judith, I do." It was an apology.

"I like to feel you touching me," she said contentedly. "That's the nicest thing of all."

He held the palm of his hand against her hot forehead and thought of people who have the power of healing. He willed himself to have that power.

That afternoon he tried to set off on one of his voyages to his distant island, but although time was passing peacefully, and there was no sound to disturb him but the monotonous trickle of water coming from somewhere in the mysterious depths of the earth to run out of the rusty pipe and into the everyday world, he still could not manage to get any further than the Customs.

"Your papers, please," said the Customs man. Peter held Judith's hand and felt her trembling with apprehension. Dear God, the man didn't even have to look at her forged passport or her dyed black hair to know there was something wrong! A suspicious Customs man is as dangerous as a policeman. Peter saw him discover the false bottom of a case with a layer of banknotes taped inside it; with a perverted kind of pleasure, he asked, "And what's all this?" As if he couldn't see they were Swiss banknotes . . .

He wondered how many tranquilizers you'd need to take so as not to arouse a Customs man's suspicion. He wondered what extortionate price Gugu would ask for the forged passport . . . the bastard. Originally he had not planned to go back to Germany at all, but now he'd have to. For Judith's sake. For her, he'd do anything, sacrifice everything. Everything? Never lose you . . . you'll never lose me, because I won't lose you . . . you do believe me, don't you . . . He tossed and turned in the hay so much that she noticed.

"What's the matter? You're not ill too, are you?"

"I'm thinking of that fool with the dog," he said, and saying it made him realize that ever since the morning he had not really managed to rid himself of the thought of them. He had been restless and edgy all day, and now he knew why. Suppose that shepherd tells someone what he saw in the barn, he thought, suppose he tells anyone who's heard of the hold-up in the Zürich store, or read about it in the papers, the fuzz will be here tonight. A hot wave of alarm flowed over him, instantly succeeded by a sense of bitter disappointment. He felt he had been lured into a trap by Fate. Fate in the shape of a stinking shepherd and his lousy dog. Or Fate in the shape of a tiny virus in the blood-stream? Or Fate in the shape of a blonde girl?

As if she had guessed his thoughts again, Judith said, "Perhaps we ought to leave here. I'm feeling much better now."

"You're just saying that," he said dubiously.

"No, it's true. I never tell lies."

"I know. I believe you," he said. He did.

"Well, just once I did lie to you, only a little."

He waited to hear what the lie was.

"I told you I was eighteen. I'm really seventeen. I added a year because I was afraid you'd look down on me."

He laughed, a boyish, carefree laugh again, as if he did not have forty-eight thousand francs in his ruck-sack, and the sun was shining outside and it would be warm for ever and ever. She couldn't see why he thought it was so funny.

"That makes two of us!" he explained at last. "I lied to you too! I added on a couple of years—for exactly the same reason!"

Then they both laughed together for the first time in ages.

They decided to spend one more night in the barn and set off early next morning. Judith's temperature had gone down, and Peter's ankle felt much stronger. They were sure they would be able to limp down the mountain-side. Peter would buy some black hair dye, and then, somewhere in the forest, they would cut her hair and dye it black. They'd buy two tickets to Geneva, where they would find a hotel where no one was particular about the papers of a young lady going to bed with a young man. There must be plenty of hotels like that in Geneva. Then they'd spend a couple of days in Geneva, or perhaps a week or even a fortnight. After that, Peter would go to Germany and come back with Judith's passport. Then they'd go on to Marseilles, or Genoa, and cross the blue ocean on a white ship . . . On and on and on they went, and then came back to the barn. He heated a can of goulash and made some tea.

After their supper, which Judith had hardly touched, they lay side by side in the hay. Outside, the wind had risen, and distant thunder could be heard far away. From time to time lightning flashed through the dark sky. Judith hugged him tightly and whispered, "I've always been frightened of thunderstorms, but I don't mind anything with you."

He stroked her hair in silence. He felt strong; he felt more important than he had ever been in all his life. Excitement flared up in him again, communicated to him by Judith's body, passing by way of his fingers into every cell of his body. But gently kissing her naked breasts, slightly sticky from the dried sweat of her fever, he caught himself listening for the sound of dogs barking in the distance. A chill of fear ran through his heated body.

"We must be sensible, Judith. We must wait till you're quite better."

"Yes," she said, docile.

He lay beside her, suddenly sober and anxious, and listened to the thunder of the distant storm.

20

Distant lightning flashed through the cloudy sky almost all night long. The rumble of the thunder grew louder, and then faded again, as the storm over the horizon wandered to and fro on the rocky peaks of the mountains. But it was not that that kept them from sleeping. Judith began to cough in the night. She tried to suppress the coughing by pulling the sleeping bag up over her head, but that only made it worse, because she was left without enough air. Peter got up and helped her into a sitting position. When she sat up, she stopped coughing. She complained of dryness in her throat and a raging thirst.

It was damp and sultry in the barn, and now and then the velvety darkness was shot through by a pale flash of lightning from the electricity-laden sky. They saw the flashes through the window. In between the lightning the darkness was blacker than ever.

"Are you angry with me?" she asked unhappily.

"Christ, no! Do you think I'm that kind of a moron?" He bent down and put his face to hers.

"I've spoilt it all. I've brought you nothing but trouble," she said. "I'm just a nuisance."

He rubbed his cheek against hers. "You're a lovely nuisance!" he said gently. "I hope you'll go on bringing me trouble for the next hundred years." He closed his eyes to shut out the oppressive dark. He felt as though he were wearing a shirt too small for him. He wished he were somewhere far away, and he thought of his distant island. It did exist somewhere, that island. An island for Judith and him. An island for two. But at night, in the dark, it seemed even further off than by day.

He made a pile of hay to support Judith's back, and fetched some water in a tin can. By the dim light of the flashlight, its weak battery now almost exhausted, he lit the spirit stove to make tea. He did not want to give her cold water to drink, with her cough.

In the morning they sat on the plank bench across the two logs, feeling tired and depressed after their disturbed night. The flames of the spirit stove standing between them licked inaudibly around the pan of water. Judith had put on her black skirt and the scratched, ruined black shoes. She was wearing his pullover on top of her blouse. It was too big for her over the shoulders, and she had to turn up the sleeves.

"Do you really think you're all right to start out?" he asked doubtfully. She seemed so different now. Could this really be the girl with whom he had set out on Saturday in his old Volkswagen? A week ago . . . almost a week ago? It just was not possible that he'd known her so short a time! He'd known her for years. He knew her from his dreams. But he had only known that her name was Judith for just under a week.

"I feel fine!" she said, but it did not sound completely convincing. She was not used to telling lies, but now she thought it necessary.

In silence, he looked at her hand, with its long, white fingers, watching her try to clean the dust off her black skirt. Little bits of hay clung obstinately to the material.

"No, really, I do feel fine," she assured him. "Just a little bit frightened, that's all."

"What of? I'm with you, right?"

"I don't *know* what I'm frightened of. It's just a funny sort of feeling. Could be the aspirin."

He lifted his hand and stroked her face. He wanted to say something about their island for two, the way he had thought of it in the night, but suddenly it didn't seem quite the right moment. Instead, he said: "When we get to Geneva we'll look for a small hotel, with a small room, and an enormous great bed in it. Then I'll look after you till you've shaken off this damn bug."

The water began to hum, and threads of silvery little bubbles rose and broke on the surface. He was just going to put coffee powder into the boiling water when his hand, holding the coffee can, froze in mid-air. A shadow had fallen across the mud floor by the doorway. There was someone standing there. He must have crept up so quietly that they had not heard him. How many of them were there out there, he wondered? His heart began to thud. Somewhere far away, palm fronds swayed above the sandy beach in the warm sun, swayed in the salty wind blowing off the sea . . .

"*Buon giorno!*" said the man in the doorway, laughing. "Hope I didn't give you a fright!" he went on, in German. It was the shepherd back again.

"Why would you have given us a fright?" asked Peter, completing the movement of spooning coffee powder into the hot water. He could still feel his heartbeat in the pulse at his throat, and he tried to control his shaking hand. He managed to produce a forced laugh; that helped. He glanced at Judith, sitting with her head bent, staring at the bubbling coffee and rubbing the palms of her hands nervously over her short skirt. "The only thing we're frightened of is savage dogs!" he went on, with assumed ease. "Where's your dog, then?"

"Up there," said the shepherd, jerking his head vaguely. His eyes were riveted to the girl's long legs.

Peter noticed. Involuntarily, his face darkened. However, he'd rather this shepherd than a cop . . . he'd rather *ten* randy shepherds than a cop. He asked the man to sit down and offered him some coffee.

The shepherd took the tin can of coffee without demur, and sat down on a log. The can was hot, and he put it down on the ground to let it cool off. He looked curiously at Judith. "This place used to belong to my father," he said. He pointed to the floor with a gnarled finger. Perhaps he was making that an excuse for his visit. Or perhaps, up there with his sheep, he felt the need for human company, and just wanted to talk to someone. He jerked his head in the general direction of the door again, and went on. "But when that burned down, over there, my father sold the place and we went to Germany. In the fifties, that was. I was eighteen then. Not much work in these parts, not much money to be earned. Plenty of work in Germany, though. Plenty of money. We only stuck it out for five years, all the same. My father got ill, so we came home. He wanted to die at home, not among those Germans. He was a patriot, he was!" He gave a brief laugh. "He was lucky to die when he did! The place is full of Germans now. All Switzerland belongs to those German millionaires, these days."

Peter blew on his can of coffee, which was burning his fingers, and wondered what the hell Swiss patriots and German millionaires had to do with him. He was not listening to the shepherd as he rambled on. He was thinking of Aunt Liese and Uncle Paul. *They* didn't own villas in the south of Switzerland. All they had was one room and a kitchen, with mildewed walls which looked like maps of undiscovered continents. Their one room, which could hardly accommodate the marital bed, had no window. It had originally been a storeroom, and the kitchen had once, before the war, been a shop. It's not everyone who gets to be a millionaire. When he started work in the garage, he thought he'd make a pile too. He was still fool enough to think you could earn a lot of money just by hard work. Later, the light dawned on him. People work simply so that they can eat and sleep and clothe themselves—and be able to work. A vicious circle. You worked so that you could live, that was all. The discovery shook him badly. Somewhere or other there was a terrible mistake. He wanted to escape, break free of the circle, get out. He heard the shepherd talking, but he did not listen to what the man said. He felt sure the shepherd was a Peeping Tom who had hoped to surprise Judith and himself in the hay; that would be why he had come creeping up so quietly. That was why he had left his dog behind. No doubt he'd been peering in through a hole in the wall somewhere first—even through the window, maybe— for God knew how long!

"You're Germans too, you are!" said the shepherd, firmly.

Peter pulled himself together. "Germans, yes. Not millionaires!" He laughed out loud: forced laughter.

The shepherd laughed too. "Well, the hell with money, that's what I say! It's too much work, earning money! Even a horse'll collapse if you drive it too hard."

Judith did not laugh; she was trying to suppress her cough.

"How's the foot?" the shepherd asked her, winking. It must be a habit of his.

"The foot's fine," said Peter, "but my wife's caught a cold. She's so hoarse she's completely lost her voice." He looked hard at Judith, hoping she understood what he was trying to tell her. He didn't want the shepherd to hear Judith's accent and know she was Swiss. It hurt him to think he would have to cut Judith's long hair and spoil its lovely color with some kind of chemical muck, but it was too striking. However, he thought, if this bastard's been listening to the radio up there in his mountain pasture it's too late already. Maybe he's come to spy on us. He looked at the man's narrowed eyes as he drank his coffee, and thought he could see the sly enjoyment of a secret in them. What was he thinking about? Lovers tumbling in the hay, or a hold-up in Zürich? "What was the weather forecast on the radio?"

"I don't listen to the radio," said the shepherd. He smiled.

Peter read a world of meaning into that smile.

"It doesn't work—needs new batteries. They don't last long, not with it being so damp up here," the shepherd went on, between noisy gulps of coffee. "I don't need any radio to tell me what the weather's going to be, though. Not me. I've got my knee. An old accident, that was. When my knee hurts it's going to rain."

"How about today, then?"

"Ah, there's a storm coming today. In an hour or so. Better not get wet, not when you've got a cold." He turned to Judith and stared avidly at her feet, still gulping his coffee. The log where he was sitting was quite close to the ground, and it looked as if he were trying to see up her short skirt.

Peter felt a strange sensation on the back of his neck, like an invisible mane rising on end. Suppose this snooper had been prowling around the barn yesterday? "Our holiday's nearly over, though. We have to get home. We're from München."

"Better wait till tomorrow, if you ask me."

"Why tomorrow?" he asked suspiciously, watching the shepherd closely.

"It'll be a long storm, this one. You wait and see. It'll pass over and then come back. We'll have rain till dawn, but tomorrow will be fine. That's how they always go this time of year." He went on discoursing on the weather, and the millionaires who came to build their luxury villas here on account of it, and launched into a list of the famous actors who had houses here.

A strange, mournful light fell into the barn. It was sultry. Judith coughed now and then.

Finally the shepherd got up, thanked them for the coffee, and prepared to leave. He looked as if he were about to say something else, but did not know how to put it. He glanced at Judith and laughed, briefly and for no obvious reason. He surveyed the barn. "You're not kitted out right for a mountain holiday, though. Take my advice: another time, you bring some good stout shoes. Same as these." He kicked the log with the toe of his shoe. It was, indeed, a large, stout shoe with coarse ridges on the rubber sole; there was dried mud stuck between the ridges.

When he went, he left behind him a few bits of dry mud beside the log, and a painful uncertainty. Did the man know anything, or not? The sky outside was getting dark.

"Do we have to go now?" asked Judith, worried.

"Let's wait an hour and then see. We don't want you getting wet; the bastard was right there." He went to the door and looked long and thoughtfully at the sky.

"He wanted us to stay here till tomorrow so he'd have time to go to the police," she said quietly. "Is that what you think?"

"No, Judith. He's a Peeping Tom—someone who spies on lovers to see what they're up to. A goddam pervert, see?" He only hoped he was right. "That's why he crept up so quietly, without his dog."

Judith began to cough, holding her hand to her breast. When the attack was over, her face was flushed with the strain and she had tears in her eyes. "Do you think he saw me getting dressed?"

He looked into her eyes, deeply sunk in their blue-rimmed sockets, and he felt a sensation like a smooth, cold stone turning over in his stomach. He never had any luck. How could he have expected to be lucky this time? Judith, Judith . . .

"Doesn't matter whether he saw you or not, Judith. Any other time I'd have thrashed him till he couldn't bloody function at all—but not today. It doesn't matter today. Getting to Geneva, that's what matters."

An hour later a gale broke loose. The bushes behind

the barn thrashed about wildly, and the wind whistled through the stones on the roof. He went out and walked all around the stone building. There was a gap a finger's breadth wide at one point in the old wall. Looking at the ground, he saw the prints of shoes with coarsely ridged soles in the mud. He bent down and felt the prints; the mud was hard and dry. He put his eye to the crack, and found that he could see the sleeping bag in the light that fell into the barn through the small window. He realized that his feelings were mixed. He was glad he'd been right: the shepherd *was* a pervert, a Peeping Tom. At the same time, he was overcome by helpless rage. Looking into the space framed by the black shadow of the crack, he seemed to see a strange image of Judith's naked body and his own, moving convulsively together. He closed his eyes and leaned against the wall. There was something dirty about this wall, this place. Something that grieved him, too, whatever it was. He stood there outside the barn until a blinding flash of lightning cut through the dark clouds, and thunder rolled noisily across the sky.

When he went back inside Judith nestled against him. "I was just thinking," she said. "Thinking how dreadful it would be to be alone in the world, without you."

A squall of rain lashed the stone barn for almost an hour. Flash after flash of lightning rent the sky, and the thunder crashed incessantly. Then the storm changed to settled rain. And then the lightning came back, flashing through the wet atmosphere, and again the air quivered to the sound of thunder. At midday it was as dark as evening. The air was much cooler now; their breath condensed to vapor.

They got into the sleeping bag together. It was the only way to keep warm, and they waited there for the rain to stop. The whole world had shrunk to the tiny space of the sleeping bag. It was a world of warmth and velvety softness and peace. Everything else was chilly and hostile.

21

By late in the afternoon it was obvious that they would not be able to leave that evening. The chilly rain showed no sign of letting up. There was nothing for it but to spend another night up here and hope that the shepherd's weather forecast had been correct. They couldn't possibly set out in the rain, for Judith was having shivering fits even in the warmth of the sleeping bag. Besides, it would be easier catching a train on Saturday; trains and stations are much more crowded on a Saturday, and the bigger the crowd, the better for anyone who wants to get lost in it. However, he kept this thought to himself. Something prevented him from mentioning such problems of a criminal's life to Judith.

They had not mentioned the money for some time, either. He was taken aback, and a little surprised, when he realized this. Something had certainly happened to him. He was different, though he was not sure if it was a change for the better or the worse. Anyway, he wasn't going to think about that; too much of a strain. Time dragged slowly by in the rainy twilight.

"Do you think it's warm *anywhere* in the world just now?" asked Judith, her teeth chattering.

He did not want to talk about the hot sands of the

island either. Instead, he said, "I'll make you some tea. Plenty of hot tea—that'll warm you up."

He fetched water, and put several of the cubes of solid spirit in the bottom of the little stove at once. He wanted to get the water boiling as soon as possible, and there was no need to economize on fuel now. They'd only be using the stove once more, first thing next morning. He lit the spirit, put the pan of water on the stove, and sat down on the bench beside it.

Outside, twilight was closing in, and it was almost dark in the barn. The pale blue flames licked around the cold pan, and their orange tongues cast a faint, flickering light over the hard mud floor. Drops of water hissed on the side of the pan, and the cubes of fuel, damp from the rainy atmosphere, fell apart with a crackle. Perhaps the heat was too sudden and too strong: a piece of the solid spirit exploded like a miniature grenade, shooting bits of itself in all directions with a bang and a sizzle. One of the burning fragments flew right out of the stove, fell on the hay, and became a hungry red flame. Peter jumped up at once to tread out the flame, but his sudden movement dislodged the plank from the logs supporting it, and the little stove fell to the ground. The flames leaped out, and a whole swarm of fragments of burning spirit fell into the hay. It burned as if it had been drenched in gasoline.

Judith screamed something he could not make out. She was tugging desperately at the zipper of the sleeping bag, which she could not get undone.

He kicked frantically at the flames, trying to isolate the burning hay in an empty corner of the barn. "Get out!" he cried urgently. "Run!"

151

She finally managed to unzip the sleeping bag and crawl out. She was not wearing anything but his check shirt, and once on her feet, the first thing she did was to pick up her black skirt. But she did not put it on. She began to beat at the flames with it, which made matters worse; sparks and burning bits of hay flew up in the air and started new fires where they fell. The air was suddenly full of stifling smoke. She began to cough again.

"Run—for Christ's sake, *run!*" he shouted desperately, still stamping on the burning hay. He seized the opened sleeping bag and flung it on the blazing pile to smother the flames. But by now the fire had spread too far. It suddenly flared up by the back wall of the barn, catching the sloping beams of the roof with a roar and a crackle. Searing heat drove the acrid, smoke-filled air toward the door and windows.

Peter snatched the smouldering sleeping bag off the fire and flung it toward the door. He had a sudden fit of choking, and he saw Judith sway, coughing. In the red light of the flames, he saw her face, partly covered by locks of tangled, long hair. He ran to her, seized her hand and dragged her to the door. She staggered and fell to her knees, racked by coughing. Grasping her under the arms, he dragged her out, put her down in the wet grass, knelt beside her and smoothed back the hair from her face with the palm of his hand.

In the red glow now mingling with the blue light of evening at the barn door, he saw that Judith had closed her eyes. Her breath was labored and uneven. He bent over her and began to cover her face, her eyes and her mouth with frantic kisses. A heavy, cold rain was falling, but he did not feel it. All he could feel was Judith's warm face. Suddenly he had a terrible feeling that she might die.

"Judith!" he cried desperately. He put his hands under her head and gazed in horror at the dark cracks of her closed eyelids.

She did not open her eyes, merely whispered, "So long as we're together, nothing can happen to us . . ."

He wished this could be just a nightmare, and he could wake up and find himself beside Judith on the deck of a white ship, sailing far away on a calm sea. The crackle of burning wood behind him brought him back to reality. He made a sudden, dismayed movement, slipped his hands away from her head, and stood up. Opening her eyes, Judith sat up and saw him run back toward the door of the barn. She screamed in terror, and tried to stand up and run after him to hold him back. But she could not keep upright. Crawling over the wet grass on hands and knees, she saw him disappear inside the barn. Smoke was billowing out of the doorway. She moaned, and collapsed on the ground face downwards.

When she hauled herself up again a few moments later, she saw Peter running out of the barn, as the flames blazed up behind him. His shirt was burning. She saw him throw himself on his back on the ground and roll over and over in the wet grass to put out the flames. She crawled over to him. He was writhing and coughing, his face wet with tears and rain, his hair singed, and she saw that his right hand was convulsively clutching the strap of the rucksack that held the money.

At last he pulled himself together enough to speak. "Okay. It's okay now, Judith."

"Why did you go back in?" she cried, in a voice of mingled fear, despair and relief. "Does the money mean so much to you?"

"I did it for you," he said. His voice was calm and peaceful.

"But I don't mind about the money! Not at all!"

"I know. That's why I did it."

"I only want you."

"I only want you too. That's why! I wanted you to believe it."

"Believe what?"

"That I don't mind about the money. I love you more than a million francs—a hundred million! I'd rather have burned to death than have you not believe me."

"I don't understand," she said unhappily, "not at all. You want to be burned to death so I'd believe you love me? But I *do* believe you. You know I do."

"I know," he interrupted, "but I wanted you to believe me tomorrow too. And in ten years' time. And fifty years' time. Don't you see, Judith?"

He helped her get up, supporting her as she put her skirt on. There were several holes burnt in it. He put the charred remains of the sleeping bag around her shoulders, and then took off his sandals and put them on her bare feet.

They had to get further away from the barn; the heat was unbearable now. They stood there in the rain, close together, in silence, until the beams fell in under the weight of the stones on the roof. There was a crackle and a loud crash, and a column of glowing sparks rose into the sky. Fierce flames blazed up behind it.

"We must go," he said, in a voice she had never heard from him before.

There was more burning between the stone walls than mildewed old hay and worm-eaten wood.

Such a tiny, insignificant thing to alter the course of events so suddenly and drastically! They walked down the path to the valley in the rain and dark. They made slow progress, because he was not used to walking barefoot, and she was weak from her fever. After half an hour he began to limp badly. His ankle was hurting again. They did not talk, they merely supported each other. In the dark, he stubbed his foot against a stone, and felt a burning pain and warm blood welling out from under his toenail. But at the same time he felt as if it were not his own foot and his own body at all dragging painfully through the darkness. He was pleased to observe his indifference to pain. The rucksack on his back chafed his burns; the pain was bad, but not unbearable. In spite of his physical discomfort, he felt calmer than he had ever been before. Yes, something had changed all right. His body was the same, still vulnerable and sensitive, but something had changed inside him; he had become a different person. Suddenly he felt adult, experienced, virile. The past was ridiculous! All that was left of it was a few bundles of banknotes and an old pistol; he could feel the weight of it on his burned back.

About halfway down, at the place where the path fell steeply to the little ravine hollowed out by the stream, Judith could go no further. Her muscles, enfeebled by her illness, simply refused to obey her. He wanted to carry her. She protested, but he picked her up in his arms and tried to go on. However, it was no use; his damaged ankle would not bear the extra weight. He gave up the attempt, because he was afraid he might slip on the wet ground and fall into the ravine with Judith.

They sat down side by side on a rock to rest, and put the remains of the burnt sleeping bag over them.

"If we're together, nothing can happen to us, Judith. That's right, isn't it? You said so yourself." He pressed his face against hers. The rain flowed down their hair, which was sticking to their foreheads, rolled down their wet faces to their chins, and fell to the ground in big drops.

"So long as we're together," she corrected him gently.

He did not say anything; he knew she was right. Soon they pulled themselves together and went on again.

It was after eleven o'clock when they reached the little bridge and the road in the valley. Peter stationed himself in the middle of the road and tried to flag down a car driving toward them from Locarno at speed. The driver braked so suddenly that his tires squealed; then he swerved to avoid Peter, stepped on the gas, and disappeared into the night.

"Damn fool! I suppose he thought I was a bandit trying to hold him up!" Then he was dismayed at his own remark—he had not meant it as a joke.

He sat down beside Judith on the parapet of the little bridge, wondering how to get her into the warm as soon as possible. Get her to a doctor . . . that was it. In their singed clothes, drenched with rain, they looked such a miserable sight that a car coming from Bellinzona stopped. Peter dared not stand up for fear of alarming the driver. Then, through the darkness, he saw that the car was full. *"Cos'è successo?"* asked the driver, winding down his window.

"We need a doctor," said Peter. He did not venture to go right up to the car.

"An accident?"

"No, we've been in a fire. Burnt out."

"Dio mio!" said the driver. He went on, in German, "You're in luck. There's a doctor quite near. First villa on the left. I'll take you."

Turning to the interior of his car, he said something. The car door opened and a young man got out, followed by a girl who immediately put up her umbrella.

Peter and Judith climbed in. Only when they were inside the car did they realize how strong the smell of burning clinging to them was. The driver turned and drove back to the nearest houses. Their lights were warm in the cool and rainy night. "How did it happen?" he asked. His companion half-turned and looked at Judith with mingled sympathy and curiosity.

"Our spirit stove exploded," said Peter, wishing he need not talk.

"Porcheria!" exclaimed the driver. He said no more. He drew up at the first villa. "Dr. Egli practices in Bellinzona, but this is where he lives. He's getting on now, but he's a good doctor."

They thanked the man and got out. As the driver turned, they limped toward the gate in the garden fence. Warm light shone from a standing lamp with a golden-yellow lampshade in a big window on the ground floor. There was a faint red glow in a first floor window too. They knew this villa. A white Ford Mustang with a scratch all along one side was standing outside the garage.

22

A moment or so after they rang the bell, a man of about sixty-five opened the door. He was quite small, but very upright. He had white hair cut *en brosse,* and though it was so late in the evening he wore a white shirt and dark tie under his casual jacket. When he saw the barefooted young man in his singed and ragged shirt, supporting a pale, slender girl in a tattered skirt, with big man's sandals on her bare feet, he opened the door wide and said in Italian, "Come in. What's happened to you?" He sounded calm and matter-of-fact.

"There was a fire. But that doesn't matter. My . . . my friend's got pneumonia. She needs a doctor."

The doctor smiled indulgently. "And how do you know your friend has pneumonia?" he asked in German, with a strong Zürich accent. He led Judith through the hall, over Persian rugs, into the sitting room. "I don't have a surgery here, but I'll see what I can do."

In the bright lamplight he saw the expression in the girl's eyes for the first time, and he frowned. "Good God, how did you get into this state?" Taking her by the arm, he led her over to a divan with several small cushions on. "Wait in the hall," he told Peter.

Alone in the hall, Peter was overcome by a dismal

feeling of loneliness. He looked at the pictures in their ornate gold frames, staring blankly at some face that stared impassively back from the wall at him. Who was the old lady with the double chins? Why was her picture here? Was she the doctor's mother? Someone nearer and dearer? He tried to remember what his own mother looked like, but he could only visualize a dim, vague outline. Everything from his distant childhood seemed gloomy and ill-defined. Why the hell should *I* take in her bastard . . .

The tall grandfather clock in the corner of the hall ticked loudly. Its long pendulum, behind the glass door, swung slowly and deliberately from side to side. He bent his head and looked at his bare feet. There was blood encrusted around his big toenail. The Persian rug beneath his feet was soft and silky. This was another world.

He heard someone coming down the wooden staircase leading from the hall to the second floor. A young woman, possibly the doctor's daughter; she wore a flowered pink dressing-gown. A bit of her black bra was visible in its deep cleavage. Peter said, "Good evening," feeling embarrassed. She replied in a chilly tone, looking the young man up and down from his head to his bare feet. Her voice sounded cross and edgy.

"Even a doctor has a right to his weekend, you know!" she informed him. "People who get into drunken brawls are a matter for the police, not the doctor."

At any other time this remark would have annoyed him. In normal circumstances he would have been angry, but not today. Today everything was different. He stood barefoot on the Persian rug, the pistol and the forty-eight thousand francs in the canvas rucksack at his feet, and he could hear coughing in the next room. He didn't want to speak. He didn't want to defend himself. His eyes traced the pattern of the rug. He heard the woman close the door behind her. The cow, he thought. The stuck-up cow.

It seemed an eternity before the doctor came out of the sitting room, closing the door after him.

"Why didn't you come before?" the doctor asked sternly.

He felt the smooth, hard stone turn in his stomach. "Is she bad?" he asked in a strangled voice.

"I'm afraid your diagnosis may have been correct. I must get her into the hospital."

"Is it very bad?" He tried hard to keep his voice under control.

"It could be. I've given her an injection. But we must get her to the hospital. Why didn't you come before?"

"We couldn't. It wouldn't have been any good," he said. He hunted for words for a few seconds, and then got out: "I'm a bandit, you see."

The doctor looked at him coldly. "Is that supposed to be a joke?" he said dryly.

"It's not a joke." He bent down and took the pistol out of the rucksack. "Now do you believe me?"

The doctor looked him in the eye in silence. He showed no fear or horror. They stood facing each other. The slow ticking of the clock was audible in the quiet of the night.

"I suppose she's the girl from Zürich?" the doctor asked wearily. "The girl who was in the papers?"

"That's right," he said, dully. Again there was no sound but the ticking of the clock.

The doctor looked at the pistol lying on the young man's hand, its gleaming shape reflecting light from the wall bracket. "What are you going to do now?"

"I'd like to say goodbye to her," he said. "Can you arrange about getting her into the hospital?"

"Of course." He stepped back from the door to let the young man through.

"And there's something else I'd like to ask you. I don't think you'll mind." There was a trace of bitterness in his voice.

"I will do anything that is not against my conscience," said the doctor coldly. "Even though you are speaking from a position of strength, as they put it these days."

"Position of strength!" he repeated. "I was never in that kind of position, only dreamed of it, that's all. You can't actually shoot with this pistol, see?" He picked up the rucksack, opened the door, and went into the room.

The old doctor hesitated for a few moments, undecided, and then followed him.

Judith was lying on the divan, covered up to her chin by a checked woollen blanket. The big, wet sandals with their muddy heels looked incongruous on the shiny parquet floor. Her eyes were closed.

"Judith!" he said softly.

She started as if she were waking from a dream, and an apologetic smile formed on her lips. "I thought you'd be gone by now." Her voice was weak and expressionless. Then she saw the pistol in his hand. The smile left her face, and a mournful, sad, ill look came into her hollow eyes.

"Judith, keep calm, don't worry."

"Hurry up," said the doctor brusquely, from the doorway. "She's ill; she needs to rest. She's had a strong injection."

"Okay," said Peter. "I won't be long." But something inside him was still fighting for life. He looked around the room. It was a big room, with antique furniture, Persian rugs, dark pictures in heavy frames, full of an ancient and quiet peace. A clock set on four little pillars stood on the marble mantelpiece of the big fireplace, and its pendulum was a gleaming disc in the shape of the sun which shone as it swung to and fro. The black figures on its white face showed that it was three minutes after midnight. A new day was beginning. A low table, its top inlaid with wood of different colors, stood under the golden-yellow standard lamp by the deep armchair. On the table lay a folded newspaper, and on top of the newspaper a pair of glasses. He went up to the table, pushed the newspaper aside, and put the pistol down on the polished wood. Then he turned the rucksack upside down and shook out its contents. The pistol disappeared under bundles of banknotes.

"I wanted to go somewhere far away, you see," he said. His own voice sounded strange to him. "I just wanted to get away—a long way away—do you understand?" he asked insistently.

The doctor looked silently at the heap of banknotes. "I understand."

"No, you don't!" he cried bitterly. "How could you understand?" Something was constricting his throat so that he couldn't breathe. He felt his heart pulsing there. At last he managed to draw a breath, and he heard himself saying, "Call the police."

"Oh, yes, I understand," said the doctor. His voice was calm, but it sounded weary. "I understand it all. The fact is, I always thought bandits were rather different."

"I thought you'd be different too," said Peter mechanically. "Looking at that Mustang of yours." He was not really thinking of what he was saying; his mind was on other things. It came out because that was what he had been thinking when the doctor opened the door to them.

"Ah, that's not my car; it belongs to my wife. We imagine so many things to be different from the reality," said the doctor, going out of the room.

Peter went up to the divan and bent over Judith. He grimaced with pain as the burnt skin on his back stretched. He laid his hand on Judith's forehead.

"Oh, yes!" she whispered. "It's good this way."

He was not quite sure what she meant, but he hoped and guessed she meant everything. He knelt down by the divan, because his back was hurting unbearably, and laid his face on Judith's hand. It was good this way. With relief, he listened to the gray-haired man out in the hall dial a telephone number.

Epilogue

"Can you hear me, Judith?" he whispered. He was kneeling by the divan, his elbow propped on its side. They were alone in the room.

"Yes," she said quietly.

"Do you know why I really went back into the barn for the money?"

"Yes, I know."

"So you wouldn't think that was why I gave up," he said, just in case.

"I know," she whispered.

"Look, I want you to promise me something. Swear it!" he said, softly but insistently.

"Yes, I'll swear," she said at once.

"You must say I made you do it."

"No," she said.

"You must!" he said, louder.

"No!" she whispered.

"Please. I'm asking you."

"No," she said for the third time. She did not open her eyes, but she put her hand out and touched his face with her fingers.

He said nothing for a long time. The clock on the

mantelpiece ticked gently. Then he asked, "Won't you forget me? I mean, before—before it's all over with."

"I won't forget you."

"We can go away somewhere together then. Somewhere far away."

The injection was obviously beginning to take effect. Her limp hand fell to the blanket.

He stood up, slowly. He didn't want them to find him kneeling down. All he wanted now was for time to pass as quickly as possible. To get it all over with. Automatically, he put out his hand and picked up the newspaper lying beside the heap of banknotes. It was a German paper, from Zürich dated 26 June, 1972. Tahiti. Why did that name jump out at him, just now? There it was, in large, clear print. TAHITI. He read a few lines, and threw the paper back on the table. "Bastards!" he said, under his breath. "They'd rape the whole world."

"What is it?" she said feebly.

"Nothing, Judith, you must sleep—they've let off a nuclear bomb on some island. Somewhere near Tahiti."

She was silent for a long time, and he thought she had fallen asleep, but then she spoke once more, in a voice that seemed to come from very far away.

"Was it our island?"